# LOVE OFFLINE

A story by NITESH CHORARIA

**BLUEROSE PUBLISHERS**
India | U.K.

Copyright © Nitesh Choraria 2024

All rights reserved by author. No part of this publication may be reproduced, stored in a retrieval system or transmitted in any form or by any means, electronic, mechanical, photocopying, recording or otherwise, without the prior permission of the author. Although every precaution has been taken to verify the accuracy of the information contained herein, the publisher assume no responsibility for any errors or omissions. No liability is assumed for damages that may result from the use of information contained within.

BlueRose Publishers takes no responsibility for any damages, losses, or liabilities that may arise from the use or misuse of the information, products, or services provided in this publication.

For permissions requests or inquiries regarding this publication, please contact:

BLUEROSE PUBLISHERS
www.BlueRoseONE.com
info@bluerosepublishers.com
+91 8882 898 898
+4407342408967

ISBN: 978-93-6261-804-7

Cover design: Tahira
Typesetting: Tanya Raj Upadhyay

First Edition: November 2024

# Love Offline

"Good morning, it's time to wake up". Beep beep....

The shrill mechanical voice dragged me from the world of imagination into the mundane real world. It was my stupid alarm clock, ringing at 7 a.m. Gosh!

I tried to go back to sleep and meet my princess Sunaina in the dream world again, but this time, the sound of the natural world was calling insistently my senses to wake up and get going.

"It's 7 a.m. How long do you want to sleep? Don't you have to do your daily chores and then go to the office? Wake up, Arjun!" my mom continued yelling.

It is impossible to even think of returning to meet my princess! *While it is true that you can fall back to sleep despite a ringing alarm clock, you definitely can't if your mom is the reason!*

It was an exciting day for me, one I had been waiting for a long time. I was supposed to meet the girl whom I had not even seen thus far, my online-cum-offline friend Sunaina. The clock had raced to 8 by the time I finished breakfast. The scheduled time to meet her was 11 a.m. at CCCD near Indiranagar. It sure wasn't a great place to meet my unknown beauty for the first time, but as a Marwari guy, I was bound to think about money first.

I was all ready to leave and come face to face with this beautiful girl. Of course, my imagination assured me she was the most beautiful girl on the planet. She had crashed into my life a year back. I remember leaving home with my Honda Activa because Dad had denied me the opportunity to take his SUV. I kick-started the 2-year-old scooty and re-entered my world of imagination. All that was buzzing in my head right now was Sunaina.....

I met her on Yahoo Messenger after my first heartbreak.

# Chapter – 1

*One Year Ago...*

"Let's go to some pub in Koramangala," Ankit suggested.

I was silent. Not all the time I used to, but today I was. I had the first breakup of my life. A group of intelligent friends surrounded me and consoled me when Ankit came up with another disgusting idea.

"Yeah," Vicky supported Ankit. *It's typical of boys. If you're sad, they will ply you with a drink. If you're happy, you have to offer them drinks. In either way, you end up being drunk.*

"It's OK buddy, even though I had a breakup two months back, but now you see how happy I am" Vicky flaunted. The asshole has uncountable girlfriends, but none of them are serious. He only knows how many times he slept with his ex.

"Ok, let's go to Man U Bar". I know it's not going to heel me, but I was happy that I wouldn't get any more stupid ideas.

"Two large whiskeys & one beer," I placed my order with the bartender. He was looking at me as if he was trying to figure out what had happened to me.

"Heartbreak!" He slowly whispered.

"Yeah," I was amazed at how the bartender and your friends learned that you had just experienced heartbreak.

"Don't try whiskey; instead, take this mocktail. It will soothe you".

I was already messy, so I preferred not to argue. I placed my order, as did my other friends.

"Leave it, Arjun. Forget her. She was a gold digger". This time, it was Ritesh, another *tharki* of the group. He preferred to be called Ritz, as it sounds macho and fashionable.

"Yeah, it was her bad luck; she will soon be punished," Satyam predicted. Like his name, he was the saint of our group.

I was literally in no mood to speak to anyone. Riya, whom I loved the most, had just kicked me out of her life because she felt it was impossible for me to accomplish her dreams.

I won't say it was her mistake completely; even my weakness to against my family led this to happen. My intelligence group warned me not to go into a relationship with Riya since she is too ambitious and will find it hard to settle in a traditional Marwari family. But I couldn't resist. Her charm didn't let me go off. Maybe it was true that love is blind, but nobody said love is also deaf.

Riya, no doubt, was an ambitious girl. We were in the same tuition for C.A course. I still remember when I saw her for the first time, entering the class. Heavy rain drenched her. Her Mustard coloured suit was glued to her body. Her wet hair could quickly get an instant proposal for ads. She was like a damsel. I still couldn't believe that beautiful girls also do one of the most challenging courses in India – C.A.

My entire group of friends used to ogle at her, as she was the only girl in the whole class who was so charming. Okay, I admit, she was an eye candy. Every guy wished Riya to sit by his side, but her group of girls always surrounded her. Needless to say, none of them deserved to be her friend even. Unlike other guys, my wish came true.

One fine day, I came too early in the class & reserved the first row for my friends. Suddenly, I saw a female shadow appearing. She was adjusting her hair. The tip-top sound of her sandals increased my heart-beats. It was Riya. I couldn't believe, we were alone in the class.

"Hi, Arjun," Riya greeted.

"Hi, Riya, you came so early?". *I realized it was the stupidest line I had just said.*

"My friends are coming late today, so they asked me to reserve their seats in the front row, but I guess I'm late" she sighed.

"Not at all; I am not reserving the seats for anybody," I lied.

"Really! I thought you were reserving these seats for your bunch of friends?'

"I am not sure whether they will come".

"Okay, thanks a lot for giving the front row," she giggled.

That was the first time I observed her lips so closely. It was looking smooth. The light pink lipstick with gloss added colour to her beautiful lips. I instantly wanted to kiss her. Somehow, I controlled. Her bunch of friends arrived no soon, & interrupted the lovely conversation.

"Hi, Riya," her friends greeted in unison.

"Hi guys, you're fortunate today. Arjun shared his first-row reservation with us".

"Thanks, Arjun," they smiled.

I was feeling good till the time I saw my intelligence group coming. They saw me sitting in the first row with Riya, so they preferred the last bench of the class. My group was known as LLB. Not because we were doing

LLB or because our fathers were LLB. It was a short name for "Lord of the LAST Bench".

Class began in no time. Suddenly, I heard a chorus in a soft voice – "Dost Dost naa raha...."

"Your order, sir," Bloody bartender disrupted my memories.

"Ah, thanks, bud." Ankit was delighted to see his order. I, too, picked my order. The mocktail was yucky, but I had no option. The sorrow of the breakup with Riya and the pain of payment for such an expensive cocktail made me sicker.

"Arjun, you can find another girl too," Vicky advised.

"Yeah, you will get one easily. Just forget her, who didn't care about you and your feelings," Ankit supported while taking a sip of Jack Daniel's 12-year-old whiskey.

"Buddy, you need to get over this, or else you will not be able to concentrate on campus placements which shall happen next month. We barely have ten days to prepare," Satyam made some sense.

"Yeah, by the way, which company are you planning?"

# Chapter – 2

"Which company will you opt for during campus recruitment?" Riya asked me while sipping her mocha. We both cleared our CA in the first attempt.

"You already know it, Riya. I am not going to sit for campus recruitment. I have my family business, which is running well, and I can take it to another level".

Riya didn't belong to any industrialist family, so she was least aware that you have no right to say anything to your elders when you belong to an Industrialist family.

"Why don't you want to join?" she banged the table. "Even you can use the corporate exposure in your business, right?" I couldn't figure out whether she was seeking my opinion or pushing me to say she was right.

"Riya, why do you want me to get a job? I am already well-settled," praising my family for being wealthy.

"Well-settled?" Riya exclaimed as if she didn't know about my family background. "Arjun, you're not well-settled. You are enjoying the wealth that your father earned for you through his hard work. What are you going to give to your next generation? Why don't you want to stand on your own?"

"Not again, Riya," We had this sort of argument like million times since she became my girlfriend.

"Fine, you enjoy your wealth; I will leave".

Before I could say anything, she left with an angry look. I knew, this time, it would take a very good long time for me to cool her down.

*"Tringg...Tringg...The person you're trying to reach is not taking your call; please try after some time".*

It was my 30$^{th}$ attempt to speak to Riya. I didn't take even 1/10$^{th}$ of it to clear my CA. Gosh! It's too challenging to light up the mood of a beautiful girl.

Finally, I heard a beep sound. It was my message tune. I checked & prayed. It was Riya, with an order. "I want to meet you now in Forum Mall".

I was happy, but I feared, what was going to happen next.

I was punctual. We met in our favourite place, McB. We occupied our place and ordered Veg Meals.

"Arjun, I can understand; you have a family business. But you should also think that working in some corporate house will give you an idea of how to manage an organization," Riya was making sense; may be the burger was speaking.

"I know, but it's tough to convince them," I munched on my burger.

"If you can't fight for yourself, how will you support me? You know I want to do a job after marriage, too".

My family knew about Riya, but they rejected her *job-after-marriage* scenario. "I will persuade them to let you do the job after marriage."

"If you can't persuade them for yourself, I find it hard to believe you will persuade them for me. I don't want money, but I want respect. I don't want people to know me as Daughter-in-law of Singhania's but as Riya Singhania". I could easily figure out her frustration, but I was helpless. For the first time in my life, I cursed myself for being born into a wealthy family.

"Arjun, we have been in a relationship for the past two years. We love each other a lot. Now, it's up to you where you'll take our relationship?". I was surprised by the question she asked me.

"Means?" I was sipping the last shot of my Coke.

"It means if I don't get permission to work after marriage, I'm afraid we have to part ways". I couldn't believe she just said it. We had fights on several occasions, but we never threatened like this.

"What are you saying? Are you nuts...?" I almost shouted.

"I am in my senses. I need you to be in your senses soon. I will wait for your reply," Riya left.

I wondered why this girl wanted to work, even though she was marrying a guy who could, or better to say, whose family wealth can fulfil all her desires.

I engulfed the last bite.

# Chapter – 3

Somehow, I finished my glass of mocktail. All my friends were busy choosing the list of companies to apply for, and I was thinking of revenge. I don't know with whom I should take it out: my family who didn't support me; Riya who didn't understand my situation; or myself, who couldn't do anything even though I could have.

"So, where should we head now?" Ankit asked as if he was in perfect condition to go anywhere.

"I will go to Gurinder ji's Café; what about you guys?' I said.

The rest of the group decided to go to a nearby park. I headed for the cafe. The cafe was barely at a distance of 15 minutes through a dark lane. When I entered the dark lane, memories of Riya haunted me. Tears were flowing from my eyes inconsolably. I sat on the pavement and cried out loud. I remembered my first lip-lock with Riya in this dark lane. She was too afraid to come, but I convinced her. I still vividly remember; she was feeling shy when I hugged her tightly. Even in the darkness, her face was glowing. I gently pushed her against the wall when she asked, "What are you up to, Mr. Arjun?" "Just some mischief," I teasingly said. Her lips were the most beautiful thing I have ever seen. I held her waist and pulled her towards me. Her hands were on my shoulder. We could sense both of us were breathing heavily. We came close to each other. Only an inch distance between our lips was left. I kept my hand on her left breast and locked her lips with mine. With time, it intensified. It was the first lip-lock of my life.

I got up, & kept moving till I reached the cafe. All the time, Riya's memory was with me. After reaching the cafe, I searched for Gurinder *Paji*, the owner of the cafe. The personality of Gurinder *Paji* always fascinated me. The guy was around his forties but popularly known as 'Muscle Man'. He was around 6 feet tall, with excellent physique. Looking at him, anybody could say he was regular to the gym. The way he wears his turban is neat. Looking at his wrist, I always feared if such a wrist hit my face, I might end up losing 2 to 3 teeth.

"Arjun *Puttar*, what are you looking for?"

"Nothing *Paji*, just wanted a system for an hour".

He made an entry in his register, & took my PAN card number, as it was necessary to show any valid ID card for using Cyber Cafe's system.

After entering the details, *Paji* assigned me a system in the extreme corner. The good thing about this cafe was that each system had a separate cabin with a seating capacity of two people. I went into the cabin and closed it.

Tears were still flowing, but I controlled. The only reason I came to the cafe was to stay alone for some time. I browsed the screen and saw Yahoo Messenger. I logged in and went to a chat room. All the people were either busy flirting or using slang. The girl's ID used to say Hi, & hundreds of Hi would come from the male ID. I don't know why the sex ratio was so poor, like 1:100. I scanned the IDs of people in the chat room. I started pinging on girl IDs randomly.

"Hi, Arjun this side"

"Hi, Sunaina here"

"You have a lovely name. May I know where from you are, Sunaina?"

"Myself from Mumbai. What about you?"

"Bangalore".

"I know it's wrong to ask a girl's age, but if you don't mind, may I know your age?"

"Next week, I'll be celebrating my 24$^{th}$ Birthday. What about you? I know, it's not an offense to ask a guy's age".

"Yeah, true. It's 25".

"What u do, Sunaina?"

"Fashion Designer. What about you?"

"Chartered Accountant by profession."

She then told me that her father and brother are also CA. Somewhere, I felt good. After all, it was one of the toughest and respected courses.

After an hour of chit-chat, we agreed to add each other on Yahoo. I bid her goodbye and logged out. Somewhere, I was feeling light after chatting with her.

I decided to go back home but was trembling to go. What if memories of Riya haunt me again? So, I decided to spend one more hour in the cafe. I informed *Paji*. I logged in to Yahoo once again.

"Ah! What a surprise, Mr. Arjun returned so early 😜?"

"I was about to leave, but thought it would be better to spend time with you, rather than spending with my family 😜"

"Who all are there in your family?" I enquired.

"Mom-dad, an elder CA brother, and of course myself".

"Nice, small family, Happy family"

"What about your family?" Sunaina questioned.

"Unlike yours, mine is a joint Marwari family. My father and mother, three uncles and aunties, and their kids."

"Ohh, that's nice"

"So, when did you clear your CA?" Sunaina started googling me.

"In this attempt," I said proudly.

"Oh, nice. My brother also cleared up this attempt. Was it your maiden attempt?"

"Yeah," I felt proud of myself.

"Oh, great yaar, my brother cleared in his third attempt".

"Congratulations to him".

"Thanks"

"So, which company is he planning to choose for campus?" I enquired, so that I may also get some tips and choose a centre for the campus accordingly.

"He is not going for campus recruitment. He is going to join my dad's CA Firm. Anyways, which company you'll be applying for?"

"Still figuring".

"What?" Her expression made me scared

"Campus recruitments will close in the next ten days, & you're still thinking!!!!"

"Yeah, actually I was a bit disturbed, so I couldn't concentrate," I said.

"Why? What happened?" Her curiosity was raised.

"Nothing. It's a bit personal" I sounded like a *Khadus Aadmi*.

"Oh, I see, sorry"

"Don't be sorry yaar, there is no fault of yours," I tried to be modest.

I didn't realize that an hour passed so quickly. Somewhere, I felt relieved that I had diverted my mind.

"I have to leave now. Will talk to you soon" I waved a final goodbye.

"Can we chat tomorrow at 7 pm?" She responded.

"Whenever you say, Mademoiselle," I replied with a wink.

"Okay, then I will meet you tomorrow at 7. Don't be late. Buh-bye," she signed off.

I logged out of Messenger &, then, the cabin. I paid the cafe charges and bid good night to *Paji*.

I checked the mirror of my scooty; I had a soft smile.

# Chapter - 4

"Where were you, Arjun? You know, today, Shruti called up to congratulate you. She just landed in London. You know she has opted for an MBA at University of London" My mom said it all in a single breath.

Shruti was my dad's childhood friend Rohan uncle's daughter. In our childhood days, we lived in the same apartment. But later Rohan Uncle shifted his business to Mumbai. So, we remained just friends.

"OK, but why had she gone to London? She could have done it in some good IIM itself," I asked in a surprised tone.

"Oh, you just don't get it. Do you know how good it feels to say that my daughter is studying in London," she said with a sparkling smile.

I could sense something fishy was going on. The day I cleared my CA, everybody in the house talked about Shruti. But I had no mood to get into any discussion, so I made an excuse of being tired, & went to my room.

There was complete silence in my room. It was still dark. My heart was still heavy. Although I had a good time with Sunaina, I realized that no matter how much

I tried, it was hard to forget Riya. I was cursing my inner strength for being so weak. I could have convinced my family, but I felt weak. Tears were still flowing from my eyes.

*Knock! Knock!*

I opened the door; Mom was there.

"Why haven't you switched on the lights? Before I could say anything, she switched on the lights.

"You're crying" She was good at figuring out what was wrong with me.

"No, it's just some dust" I tried to escape.

"There is no dust in Singhania villa. Please don't make an excuse. Say, what's wrong with you," she asked politely.

"I can't forget Riya, Mom. I always wanted her to be my life partner. She understands me better. Now when she is gone, I feel somebody has sucked the life out of my body" I cried again. This time, in front of my mom.

"It's OK. You can still get thousands of Riya, but she will never get an Arjun Singhania again."

"Mom, maybe you're right. Or it may be vice-versa. She may get thousands of Arjun, but I may not get Riya Sharma again," I replied carelessly.

"I don't know what you have seen in that girl. If it's about beauty, many girls out there are more beautiful, charming, and intelligent than Riya. Why you're so sticky to Riya? What's there with her?" Mom asked angrily.

"Self-respect," I uttered.

"Hi, Arjun". I heard the sweet voice of a girl on the other side. It was morning 6. It wasn't very pleasant to be awake so early, but if a girl wakes you up, you almost get squared.

"Who's this?" I was trying to catch up.

"I knew you would forget me. How could you be so dumb, Arjun? Shruti here," she fumed.

This time, I was in a complete sense. I knew her anger very well.

"Oh, hi, Shruti, how are you? Heard you're in London for an MBA. Wow, so now you'll be having a foreign degree," I tried to pull her legs.

"Very funny, Mr. CA. I tried for colleges in India, but Dad insisted I go to London, & study there," She reverted.

"Oh, that's cool. So, how's London?"

"Amazingly beautiful. I wish I never return to India."

"Ok, then get married to some NRI or any English guy. With a foreign degree, you'll get a foreign hubby too," I laughed.

"Stop pulling my legs, I am no more that little shy Shruti, ok".

"Ok, Ok, no more leg pulling".

Shruti was a good friend of mine. We had a great time in our childhood. Our bonding was cool. I didn't realize we had a tele-talk of more than an hour.

"Hey Mister, I have to go now. I will see you later. Need to sleep now. Goodnight to me, & Good morning to you. Bye Arjun, take care," she finally hangs up after 01 hour 04 minutes 38 seconds. Thanks to mobile, which makes you realize at the end of the call how much time you have invested in the person.

My day begins with a lot of noise in the house. Sometimes, it seems to be a fish market in the morning. Everybody is busy with the headlines of the Economic Times and Business Standard. Which stock would go up, and which stock would fall? I was least bothered by such a gamble.

I was done with my breakfast. Suddenly, my phone beeped. It was a notification. When I saw it, I knew I was in trouble. It was Ankit's birthday. *You know, there are few people in the world who expect you to be the first one to wish them on their memorable occasions. One of them is your best friend.*

"Hi Ankit, wishing you a very happy birthday," I was expecting some thrashing as I wished him.

"You jerk, is it the time to wish your best friend on his birthday? I got Riya's wish before yours," he shouted, but in a moment, he was silent.

"Riya wished you?" I was clueless.

"Err...Yeah, she called me up an hour ago. After wishing, she asked me about you. I said you're fine," he responded.

"Who the hell is she to ask about whether I am OK or not," I busted.

"Listen, buddy, I know it hurts you. But you have to accept it. She is no longer with you. You have to move on. You know you can get many other Riya Sharmas well," He consoled me.

"Can I get this one back?" I was expressionless.

"Leave about Riya; I am throwing my birthday party at Desi Messy pub. Be there at 7:30 pm sharp. And please, don't be late. This time, you don't have the excuse of a girlfriend also" He teased me.

"Asshole" I silently whispered and kept the phone.

I was feeling uneasy after the call. Why did she call Ankit to check whether I was alright? Does she still love me? Or it's just my illusion? *God damn,* girls are so unpredictable.

It was six in the evening. I was ready for the birthday bash of Ankit. I never missed his party. He always tries out something different. I was anxiously waiting for the new drink. I felt, something I was forgetting. I tried to recall and finally remembered. I have to inform Sunaina about my absence from the chat tonight. I was in two minds. Why should I inform her that I won't be available for a chat tonight? Who is she? What relation do I have with her? But at the other soft corner, I felt the need to inform her. She made me smile, which none of my friends could do after my breakup. I logged into my system. I left a message for her. *Hi, Arjun here. Sorry, I won't be available for a chat tonight. I am going to my friend's birthday party. Have a great time.*

"So, what's new today?" Ritz was too excited.

"Just wait guys. This drink will blow your mind off" Ankit replied.

We all knew the capacity of Ankit. So, we could assume tonight's drink will surely be a hangover for many of us.

"What can I get for all you handsome guys in this perfect, beautiful evening?" A husky voice came from behind.

I saw a handsome guy standing with his hands folded in front. A black-suited guy, about six feet tall, with a muscular physique. By looking at this guy, nobody could say he was a bartender.

Ankit took him aside and whispered something in his ear. A smile appeared on their faces. I knew something was going to be fishy. We were all set for the roller coaster ride.

"What you ordered, drunken fellow?" Satyam was anxious after seeing their expression.

"As I said, this drink will blow you down today" Ankit was trying to act smart.

"Your order Sir. 5 shots of absinthe" the bartender appeared.

"What the........F?" Vicky couldn't control.

"What happened, Vicky?" My jaw was still open after seeing Vicky's vivacious expression.

"Do you know, what the hell this drink is?" Vicky's expression made me scared.

"I have no idea. Why you're so afraid?" I was controlling my tension.

"This drink has an alcohol level of around 72%. One of the deadliest drinks," Vicky described.

"What?????" Now it was my turn.

The last we tried was Chivaz Regal 12 years old, neat shots. It was soothing. Later, I came to know, the alcohol level in Chivaz was around 42%. And this drink was having 72%. I could very well imagine how I would drive back home.

"Chill guys. Check this out" Ankit took the drink, and in one gulp, it was empty. He took a sugar cube to bear the burn of the drink.

His expression scared us more. Somehow, we managed to engulf it. It was terrific. From throat to stomach, we could feel the burning sensation.

"Now, what's the game plan?" Vicky playfully asked.

"Round of absinthe will go on until one of us pukes" Ankit shared his game plan.

"Please guys, leave it. It's too horrible. I can't take the another shot" Satyam surrendered.

"It's my party. So, you have to follow my game plan" Ankit left no ground for Satyam to hide away.

"OK guys" Satyam surrendered.

4 more rounds of absinthe continued. I broke the chain. I rushed to the washroom.

"Hell".

I returned to the table.

"You're OK?" Ankit expressed his concern.

"Yeah, feeling better" I was still trying to get consciousness. The music was running high. It was an old English-style pub. Lights were dim. There was a little dance floor where a few couples were tapping their feet on the electrifying music's beats. For me, it was an ideal place to get drunk.

"Let's move" Ankit paid the bill.

"Shall I drop you to your place?" Vicky put an arm around my shoulder.

"Thanks buddy, but I'll manage" I replied.

We all left in our respective vehicles. Somehow, I reached home safely, along with my dad's car.

By the time I reached my room, the clock was ticking at eleven. I was feeling drowsy. Maybe the drink was showing its effect. I retired to bed. As soon I closed my eyes, I went into a flashback.

"Hi Riya"

"Late. By 20 minutes. When shall you start being punctual, you know I hate it when you're late, especially when we are going to a movie" Riya fumed.

I knew she hated it when I was late. We were in Forum Mall for the morning show of some crap Bolly Flick. I hate bolly movies. Apart from love stories, they don't try any other subject. But it was Arman Khan's movie, so I had no regret waking up so early.

We took our seats. The seating arrangement is the main reason for watching movies along with your partner. Only two seats at each corner. These seats are purely dedicated to the lovebirds. We took our *lovebird* seat. The movie began after some boring ads.

Amid darkness in a movie hall, I held Riya's hand. It was soft and tender. I always imagined her in some ads for Vaseline moisturizer – silky and smooth skin. She held my hands tightly. But I was concentrating on the movie, casting my favourite actor, *Arman Bhai*. Within a few minutes, action scenes started. I was enjoying them like a little kid who shouts after every punch – once more, once more!

I forgot that I was with Riya. I looked at her from the corner of my eyes. She was constantly gazing at me. I knew it. The punch won't come from Arman Bhai this time, but it would be Riya. "Sorry" I slowly whispered in her ears.

"What happens to you? You really act like a kid when you watch some action movie" Riya lashed out.

I don't know, she was right, but yes, I get moved when I see some action movies. I start whistling and shouting once more, once more, just like some *tapori.*

"I don't know, but I can't control myself".

"Grow up Arjun" She got a bit cold.

"I am already grown up. You saw the trailer in that dark lane" I winked and tried to hug her.

"Easy Mister. Concentrate on the movie. You guys get wild after your girlfriend kisses" she smiled.

Even in the darkness, Riya was looking too sweet. She was wearing a Red and White *Kurti* with a matching *churidar*. Her lips were looking gorgeous in red lipstick. The perfect *kajal* in her eyes was magnetic. I was unable to remove my eyes from them.

"What happened to you, Arjun?" she brought me back to the real world.

"Nothing. I'm fine" I murmured.

"I know what you want mister" she winked.

"Then, don't make me wait"

She lifted her elbow from the side of the seat. I bent a little, hugged her, and looked into her eyes. I saw them shouting - Kiss me, Arjun, kiss me.

I brought my lips closer to hers. Suddenly, whistling and clapping sounds spoiled everything. We broke the hug and sat comfortably in our seats. Then, I learned that it was *Arman Bhai's dance.* Gosh! I missed both.

"Dad, I want to talk to you about something" I started a conversation on the breakfast table.

Like any other rich man, my dad always preferred a healthier diet ideally. A piece of cloth was hanging down from his linen shirt to avoid any spoilage to his shirt. The Rado watch added colours to the wealth. His eyes are glued to Economic Times. I wondered how these people get inside news of the company's performance.

"Say, do you want to join the office from today?" My dad didn't even look at me.

I didn't know what to say. In fact, how to say that I want to find a job for myself and earn respect and experience. I was feeling terrible at this point. *Gosh! Why was I born into a typical wealthy Marwari family? More badly, why did I do CA?*

"Dad, I want to go for campus placement," I said in a breath. *I lit the bomb; now, I was waiting for it to blast.*

"What? Have you totally lost your mind? What's the need to join some other corporate house? Why have I made such a huge business empire? Just for the sake of seeing you working for some corporate biggies at a salary in which you can't even afford your own expenses" Dad yelled. The bomb I lit made a considerable noise. All my family members gathered around the table.

"What happened?" Mom asked in a tense volume.

"This boy has lost his mental balance. He wants to join some corporate house for some penny salary. Why does he want to waste his time? Why doesn't he join my business and take it to a new height? Are we going to work forever like this?".

Emotional blackmailing was going on. Everyone supported my dad and asked me to withdraw my wish.

"Why do you want to join some other place? You can join your dad as an employee. I am sure he will pay you more than any other corporate house can give" My mom explained.

"It's not about the money, mom. It's about respect, dignity, and living on your own terms. Do you want people to always know me by my last name and not by my first name?" I shoot the bouncer. Of course, it went over her head.

"What exactly do you want to say?" My Dad yelled.

"I want to prove my worthiness. I want to see what caliber I possess? I want to gain exposure in the outer world. I don't want to stay covered for my entire life, under the surname of SINGHANIA" I made my point.

Everyone was gazing at me like I had killed some carnivorous animal brutally.

"Let him try. If he fails, our business is there to care for him" My uncle Sushant chuckled.

"What? You're supporting him, Sushant?" My dad questioned.

"Not at all. I am neither supporting him nor I am against his desire. Whatever he is saying, there is a point. You see, if he works in some other organization, and then, after some time he joins our company, he can utilize the exposure and experience he got from the other organization" My uncle played his dice.

"What do you mean to say? Are we not running this business in a sound way? Is there any loophole? We have been running this business for a generation. Not a single year I saw the face of loss. All the MNCs are reporting losses every day, cutting jobs. I don't want to see if one of the companies throws out my son. It might hamper his mental strength" my Dad counter-questioned to both of us.

Literally, I started imagining what would happen if someday my boss asked me to go home and don't turn up the next day. *Gosh! This always scares me, being called a loser.*

"But *Bhai Saab*, let us give him a chance. Else, he would complain in the future that we haven't given him a chance to prove his worthiness". By this time, I was sure my uncle was helping me to find ways.

"OK, if you people think that you're too smart than us, then go ahead. I give you exactly two years to prove your worthiness. After this, you won't get any more chances" my dad said in his verdict.

I had a sigh of relief. Finally, I succeeded in getting what I wanted. I wished Riya could be here with me to see my triumph.

# Chapter - 5

"Hi Arjun, What's up?" Sunaina greeted me.

I was thrilled. I tried to do something for myself, and I succeeded.

"Hi Sunaina 😃"

"Looking very happy, what's the reason?" she inquired.

"I will be sitting for a campus Interview. Already got the call letters from two companies - National Steel Co. Ltd. &, Ajnara Constructions Ltd. Can't tell you how excited I am" With enthusiasm, I told her.

"Wow, that's great buddy. I'm sure you're preparing hard to crack these interviews. What is your expectation?" Sunaina slapped a question for which I wasn't ready.

"Expectation? Umm... Not yet thought about it. Whatever they will pay, I would be happy" I replied innocently.

"Hahaha, you're an innocent guy. Everybody thinks about money first and then about work. Don't you have any interest in money?"

"A person who has seen wealth since childhood doesn't easily feel the aroma of hard cash. I am opting for a campus interview to prove my worth"

"Worth? Whom do you want to prove your worth?"

"To all those who felt I have got nothing. To all those people who think I can't survive if the Singhania title is taken away from me" I lashed out.

"Easy, Easy Mr. Arjun. Calm down. I am sorry for provoking you" Sunaina replied apologetically.

"Don't be sorry dear. I am sorry for misbehaving with you" I felt I was too rude to her.

"May I say something, if you don't mind?" She was too careful with her words.

"Yup, go ahead"

"Are you being challenged by someone that you don't have any worth or something like that? The way you responded, I felt somebody surely had questioned your ability"

"Yup, someone did" I took a deep breath.

"Don't worry. I know you'll prove your ability irrespective of the situation. But I have a suggestion for you. Try to control your anger; it might harm you" Sunaina advised.

"I will definitely try to overcome this issue. Thanks for your concern, dear. I have to leave now. See you later.

And once again, I am sorry for my rude behaviour" I said.

"OK dear, have a great time ahead, take care, ttyl" she replied.

I logged out. I was feeling relaxed after chatting with Sunaina. Her simplicity and patience level moved me. *What a lovely girl she is. Even though I shouted, she was calm all the time. She must be one out of the lacs - beauty with a brain.*

I checked the time. It was time for *adda*, to discuss the campus interview preparation.

"Which company offered you a call letter?" Ankit was highly excited after hearing that I would also take part in the campus interview.

"Till now, I have received call letters from Ajnara Constructions & National Steel. What about you?"

"Shortlisted by two companies – Rightwell Technologies & Bank of Patiala. I wish I could get a job at this Bank" Ankit took a deep breath.

"Why? What benefit you'll get from working with a PSU bank?" Satyam darted his anxiety.

"The only benefit of working with PSU bank is there is no working" Ankit laughed sarcastically.

"Nice say dude, but I wish if I could get a job in some MNC. High chance of foreign tour at company's cost" Vicky chuckled.

"Yeah, right. Even I wish to get into some oil company in Dubai. Heard they pay good enough, and no taxes are deducted from your pay. I could save as much in a month as my dad saves in a year" Ritz sounded genuine.

"I want to join some Audit firm. It would help me to have a good career ahead" as usual, Satyam forecasted for long run.

"I don't know guys, but I am really scared. I heard there are a lot of rounds like GD, Case laws, etc. God knows how I'm going to crack it" I let out a sigh.

"Don't worry Arjun. You'll crack it for sure. We are happy to see that you're sitting on campus. Don't take me wrong dude, but this whole Riya-dream-girl-kickass chapter brought you back to life. At least, she ignited the passion hidden in you" Ankit muttered.

"Hmmm...God knows" I was in no mood to talk about her.

"What's going on Mr. Arjun? You seem to be too busy with your campus interview preparation. Wish you luck dear. Do well" Sunaina left an offline message.

I guess it was more than a week since we had a chat. Next day was a kind of judgement day for me. Others were searching for jobs, but I was searching for my dignity. I was mentally tired now. So, to light my mood, I logged on to yahoo.

I was happy to see her wishes. I was praying that her wishes could help me out.

*Knock! Knock!*

I turned off the computer, opened the door.

"What are you doing in a locked room?" Mom asked while she entered the mini zoo. Oh, I forgot to tell. My room is a little mess. So, I prefer calling it a mini zoo.

"Nothing mom. Just preparing for my interviews tomorrow" I took my seat.

"Son, why you want to waste the time? Join your father's business. Don't you find dignity in your dad's business? He built up such a huge empire for you only. If you don't join it, your uncles may acquire it. If you want more money, he will pay you. You can work with him with the relationship of employer-employee in office. You're the only son we have. If you won't help your father, then who will help?" Mom started sobbing.

Already I was tired, after hearing all this, now I was sick. I don't know why, but I felt guilt. I felt I am selfish. Just to prove something, I was denying helping my dad in his business. Emotional scene was taking a toll on me. I was flabbergasted. I didn't know what to say, what to do. I felt like running away to some isolate place, and stay there forever.

"I know why you're doing this? This is all because of that witch Riya. Am I right?"

I was stunned to hear this. Although she was right, but not her language.

"Mom, please. Don't put Riya into this. Moreover, everything is finished between us. It was the past" I retaliated.

"Maybe you are no more in her touch, but her fragrance is still luring you. Please come out of it"

Mom left after giving her advice. I was still figuring out what happened in last ten minutes. I have lost interest into any family thing. Staying at home was making me sicker.

"Hello Ankit, can we guys meet for *adda*?"

"Sure buddy. Let's meet at tea shop near *paji's cafe* in next 15 minutes. I inform others. Ok?"

"Hmm...yeah" I disconnected the call.

"What's up? How's the preparation going on dude?" Ankit asked while taking a sip of tea.

"Just now came out of emotional drama. I don't know, why females cry out if they want something to get done. I feel like it's a weapon for them. Whenever somebody is not agreeing to their demand, pull the tears out. Quantity may vary, depending on the opposition" I blasted, without even thinking where I was standing at the moment.

All the three assholes started laughing as if I have cracked some billion-dollar joke.

"Luckily, I am not that rich" Vicky was still unable to control his laugh.

"Bro, just prays, your wife should not be as emotional as your mom. Else you will spend most of your time in your dad's office" Ritz took his sip.

I must admit, *although my friend group make fun of me when I am in trouble, they are the real buddies. I may have left them for a while for the sake of Riya, but they were always there. Even when Riya left me.*

"Feeling light now. I guess, it's the magic of the tea. I think this is also a good business. Selling tea. Profitable business. What say guys?' I winked.

"Dude, surely if we don't get a job tomorrow, we will consider this idea" Ankit replied.

We laughed together. God knows who was waiting for us behind the door. Was it the corporate slavery, or was it our tea business?

I got up early. Frankly speaking, I didn't sleep even for a minute last night. All the time I was repeating the answers in my mind. How to answer the interviewer's question, how to shake hands, how to be polite, even if the other person is kicking your butt. I wore my favourite light pink shirt with a cream-coloured tie. To match the outfit, I wore cream-coloured trousers. I was looking perfect. I felt, I could impress the interviewer with my personality. But what about my knowledge?

I decided not to think about this anymore. I took my scooty keys and left for the Ankit's place.

All the way I was thinking - what if all my other friends are selected, but not me? How will I face my family, who gave me a chance to prove my worth?

I reached to Ankit's place. Ankit was already there.

"Hey buddy, what's up? Good morning" I greeted.

"Fuck off asshole, we are already late. Stop being polite. Ride your *khatara* scooty at its peak speed"

I was prepared for such reply. I was late, as usual, by ten minutes. I rode the scooty at maximum speed and reached the venue on time.

"Hi guys" Satyam still had a book in his hand. I checked the cover properly. It was a book by some local genius about etiquettes.

"What's this? A book on etti?" I exclaimed.

"Yeah. My ride to success. This author is really superb. It tells you how to shake hands, how you should react when somebody is trying to suppress you, etc." Satyam playfully replied.

I wanted to snatch the book and read it for some time. I was damn poor in behaving socially.

"Let's go guys. The company may call out our names soon. All the very best, brothers" Ankit hurried.

"Uhh...Yeah man, wish you too all the very best" I greeted.

"Arjun Singhania. Kindly report to reception" I heard a lovely voice on the speakers. I guess my time has arrived. My heart-beats were running like *Rajdhani Express.*

"Hi, Arjun here. I was asked to report at reception"

"Hello Mr. Arjun, you have a call from National Steels. Right?" A lovely lady replied.

*I wasn't sure whether she was asking me, or confirming me.*

"Yup, I had. Have they selected somebody else, and I am being thrown out of the interviews" I spoke out in a breath. *I realized I was damn nervous. More than nervousness, I had no confidence in myself.*

"No, Mr. Arjun. They have their pattern of selection. They are making batches of ten people since they have selected several candidates for interviews. These 10-batched people will go for Group Discussion. Out of this, they might select one or two candidates. These selected candidates would then go for personal interviews. If, the number of candidates is higher than required for PI, they might add up one round before PI" She briefed me about the schedule.

"OK, so when am I scheduled for GD?" I stammered.

"In the next five minutes. Please have your seat. Wish you all the best" She replied with a beautiful smile. *Out of tension, I haven't admired her beauty. But she was looking too beautiful. White cotton shirt with Black blazer, and matching trousers with shining stilettos. She had an amazing height. Rest, I won't describe.*

I took my seat. I saw the other candidates. Some of them were reading journals. Some were watching clips on YouTube about some interesting topics. Some were chanting the name of God. I guess, CA guys remember God only a few occasions in their lives. One of them is the interview. I was shivering, biting my nails, thinking of my future whereabouts.

In a moment, a guy in a suit appeared before us. "Please proceed towards this way. It's time for your GD round" he showed the way.

We followed him in a room, where 10 chairs were kept for us. It was a kind of conference room. One middle-aged clean-shaven guy was sitting at the centre.

"Welcome all of you. You are here because National steels has chosen you people because they think you people are too competitive to take care of the dignity of the post to be offered. But we are looking for the best. As you all know, we are looking for just 10 candidates, who fit into the position very well. I request all of you to take your seats" The guy informed us about the happenings.

"I will give you a topic on which you all have to speak for about ten minutes. Remember, it's not a debate, it's a GD. Wish you all the very best" He took his chair.

"The topic for the day is Blue" He finished. *I was expecting he would say something more like blue umbrella, or blue colour, or if he is a filthy guy, he would say blue film. But to my surprise, he stopped at blue. Damn! What to say about blue?*

For a moment, there was a silence. Nobody uttered a word. Suddenly, in the next moment, it was like a fish market had opened. I could only hear multiple voices, screaming out at the same point of time. I was able to catch only one word out of the – blue.

"I hate Monday blues. It makes me realize our merry time is over, and we have to get back to work" Some echoed.

"Blue is my favourite colour. For me, it's a symbol of energy. Even team India's t-shirt colour is also blue" Some silly guy responded.

Some said blue sounds similar to blew. A guy even dared to talk about blue film. All of them were talking insensibly, just to make an impression in the eyes of the examiner, who may think at least they have contributed.

I, somehow, controlled my gigantic laugh, but the co-ordinator watched it. Everybody was putting some contribution to the topic except me. I wasn't prepared for such sort of vocal competition. I really felt miserable. I thought of contributing towards the topic, but I was scared. The way the other candidates were talking about the topic, I felt weak on my knees.

"Time's up" I heard.

I was pretty sure about my result. Others were having the zeal to know how they have performed. A few minutes later, results were declared. I quietly stood up to leave. Others have already left. The examiner called me up.

"Arjun, can I have a minute with you?" He asked politely.

"Sure, sir."

"Why were you so silent? At least you could have spoken out something. What went wrong with you?"

"Actually, I wasn't prepared for such a rushing session. I thought it would be a normal interview. I wasn't aware that a CA student could be asked to speak about a topic like Blue. I was zipped once I heard the topic. I wanted to say something, but I felt it would sound too foolish."

"What you think? Haven't you done foolishness by keeping yourself quiet? Who knows, it might have made a sense, if you would have said something?"

I felt the guy was making sense. *This word, what if, always leaves me in doubt. Whether I should go for it, or not.*

"All the very best for your career, Arjun," He wished.

"Thank you, Sir" I quietly left.

"How was your GD?" Ankit asked playfully.

It was a lunch break. We were having our lunch in a nearby restaurant.

"It was disastrous. I couldn't even utter a single word. I felt numb. The topic was blue. I didn't know what to say about it," I was feeling low.

"It was such an interesting topic. You could have talked about blue films," Vicky tried to piss me off.

"I know, you know only about these creepy things. I am serious guys. I really don't know what went wrong with me," I was on the verge of tears.

"Don't be so negative bud. You still have got one more chance," Ankit tried to cheer me up.

"Yeah, Ankit is right. Focus on the next interview. Whatever is gone, is gone. Don't commit the same mistake which you did in this one" Vicky explained.

"I will try. All the best guys. I hope when we leave this campus today, we have a job in our hands" I paid the bill & started to leave.

"All the best" Vicky cheered me.

When I returned from the lunch, I was informed that I was scheduled for PI in next 30 minutes. A candidate is in the queue before me. I went to the waiting room. I saw the other candidate. In a minute, our eyes met. A pain came down into my eyes. It was Riya.

"Hi, Arjun," she still had the same charm.

"All the best!" I replied and turned back to leave.

"Wait, Arjun. I know, you're angry with me. But can we talk for some time?" Riya pleaded.

I didn't want to, but my heart was not letting me go. I took my seat.

"Arjun, I am really happy to see you here. I don't know what you think of me. But surely, I am happy for you. You came a long way. I would be happier if you land up a job, instead of me."

"Thanks, same to you. How are you doing?" I asked

"I am doing well. I hope you have come out of the break-up shock."

"Let's not talk about it. I was never a part of this breakup. You just left me because you thought I couldn't fulfil your dreams," My anger started taking a toll on me.

"You already knew that I was ambitious about my career. Why you don't understand a simple thing that self-respect is also an important thing in life."

"Is it more important than my love?" I couldn't control this time.

"Maybe" I never expected this sort of reply from her.

"Well, then, bye have a good time," I quickly left without making an eye-contact.

"Good afternoon, Sir" I greeted while entering the room to the interviewers. I noticed it was a panel of 3 geniuses. All of them were looking above age 45.

"What is so good about this afternoon? It's the same sunlight, the same wind blowing" The guy seemed to be too frustrated. *Maybe his wife didn't cook well for him today, or may be some of my fellow friends kicked his butt in an interview earlier.*

"I know Sir. But you gave me a chance to appear before you. I feel this is the reason this noon is so good" I don't know how it came out.

"OK. Quite witty you are" I saw a narrow smile on his face. I felt positive.

"Let me introduce ourselves. Myself Assistant General Manager, Finance Mr. Anoop Tiwari. He is Mr. Pradeep Sharma, General Manager, HR. And he is Mr. Naveen Singhal, General Manager, Accounts. Now, please tell us something about yourself. A brief summary of your resume" He was getting cool.

"First of all, it's a pleasure for me to meet you all big dignities. My name is Arjun Singhania. I was born and brought up in Bangalore. My father is a businessman, and my mom is a home-maker. I have an exposure in the field of Statutory Audit, as I worked under FCA

Madan Suri, a renowned practitioner with an exposure of 20 years above. I was lucky to handle an audit team of 8 juniors under me during my final tenure of articleship. I won't say I am a workaholic, but I don't leave my work pending even a day. During my leisure hours, I play cricket, solve Sudoku & read novels" I just puked what I learnt by heart last night.

"Impressive. Even I did my article ship under Madan Sir. I was the only article, as it was a newly opened CA firm" Anoop replied. I felt I could turn at least one interviewer to my side.

"See. Our is a Construction company. And you might be aware that real sector is booming right now. Recently, we made a deal with another giant real estate biggie for technical collaboration. Can you tell me, who is it?" straight-forward question from Naveen.

"Yes Sir. It is with Ballard Estates" *thanks to Economic Times.*

"Good. How good you are in accounting standards?" Naveen went ahead.

"Competitive" I felt nervous. *As was the point where I always feel weak. Damn these AS.*

"Ok. What is the principle for accounting AS-22?" Naveen was too quick.

"Virtual Certainty supported by convincing evidence. It means there should be the feasibility of recovery for tax expenses in future" I replied.

"OK. Now tell me, what do you know about the Sub-Contractors deduction under the VAT scheme?" Naveen seemed to be interested in grilling me.

"In construction industry, it is not possible for a builder to do all the construction activity. Hence, they hire an external vendor, who can do the work on their behalf. As per VAT rules, a company is eligible for input credit on the invoice of sub-contractor to the extent which pertains to construction work" My heart was pacing like a rocket.

"OK. Tell me one thing, why do you want to do job? Your dad is a businessman. Why do you want a job in our company, rather than working with your dad?" Naveen asked.

I was numb. The whole night I was battling with this question. How I am going to face it. What should I say when an interviewer asks me this? Should I say the truth that I wanted to prove my worth, & prove my ex-girlfriend wrong, of what she thought about my capabilities? Or, should I say that I wanted to run away from my lavish lifestyle, and lead a simple and happy life?

"Arjun, what are you figuring out?" Naveen disrupted my thoughts.

"I want to work in your company and gain exposure in corporate. I may use this exposure to expand my father's business" I knew I made a mistake.

"Sorry Mr. Arjun. We are looking for guys for serious commitment for long term. We cannot go ahead with such mindset of yours. However, if you want to work with us, you may have to sign a bond with us" Naveen was really a manipulating person.

All of us were looking at him for the next blow.

"Look Arjun. Let's get practical. I liked the way you presented yourself and replied to each question. But my company has assigned a duty, in which I can't do favour to anybody indefinitely. However, I would love, if you work under me. But since you have stated your vision, I would have to take a safer stand. Any candidate we hire enjoys a goodwill. Even if he leaves our company, he gets job quickly into another company at ease. I know you're not looking for opportunities, but for an opportunity. I am willing to give it to you, the position of Assistant Manager in Accounts. But you have to sign a bond for three years. For three years, you can't leave our company. If you do so, a heavy penalty shall be imposed. What do you think? Are you willing to accept my term?" Naveen finished.

*I felt as if I was watching the movie LAGAAN, where Captain Russell asks Bhuvan for a Cricket match, and waits for Bhuvan to say – sharat manjur hai.*

A bond of three years! I felt as if he was trying to curtail my wings. I was feeling helpless. Nothing was hitting my brain. I was a checkmate.

"Sir, but three-year bond is too long. I am ready to negotiate on salary if you want, but please don't put any bond condition" I pleaded.

"Arjun, I am ready to pay you more than you expect, but the bond term will remain three years" He was too shrewd.

The others were looking as if some tennis match is going on between Nadal & Federer. Now, their eyes were set on me. They were waiting for the response. *Actually, they were looking for, who is going to win it.*

"Arjun, I know it's not an easy decision to make. Take your time, & let me know by tomorrow morning. Is it fine?" Naveen gave me a moment to breathe easily.

"Thanks Sir" I lift my ass gently, and shook hands with both the gentlemen, & a manipulator.

"I would love to see a dynamic guy like you working under me," Naveen bid me goodbye.

It was really hard to make out, whether he wants to kick my butt for the next three years, or he is simply obliging the code of conduct.

"Sure, Sir," I left the cabin.

It was the time for long breath now. I didn't know what should I do? Whether I should celebrate that I have landed a job, or I shall be sad that I will be slave for next three years. My mind was still unable to come out of the dilemma of shock and surprise. I saw a similar face approaching to me. It was Riya.

# Chapter - 6

"Hi, Arjun." She had a big smile on her face. By her expression, I got to know that she has secured a job.

"Hi" Half of my head was already heavy with such a horrific interview, and now, it was Riya, to blow the next half of my mind.

"Don't worry Arjun. If you haven't landed this job, you'll get another one. You're capable enough. Any company would love to have a genius like you". It was hard to determine whether she was making a fun of me or was feeling sympathetic toward me.

"Hmm. What about you? Where you got the job?" I asked in a husky voice.

"I landed a job in OK Bank. Guess what, my posting is in Bangalore. I have got my favourite department - Credit" She chuckled.

"Good for you" I congratulated her, and began to move.

"Can we sit for some time, in some coffee shop?" She pleaded.

"Why? You want to celebrate my defeat, or your victory?" I questioned her.

"Nope, I just want to sit with you for some time," She replied politely, which I couldn't turn down.

"Ok. Let's go to CCCD," I stood up

"What would you like to have? Mocha with Cheese Sandwich?" Riya looked upon me. *Gosh! She still remembered what I love.*

"Yup." I was trying to ignore her.

"Why you're so sad? Don't be so sad. You'll get another job soon" She was trying to motivate.

"Who told you that I haven't landed the job? I have secured Assistant Manager post in Accounts in Ajnara Constructions," I was rude.

"Hey, that's great news. Then, why is your mood so low? You should be happy that you have a job with such a big real estate player." Her eyes twinkled.

"You wanted to say something?" I interrupted.

"Arjun, can't we just remain good friends? I had some reasons to breakup with you. Please understand me. I still love you" She got emotional.

*What the F? Why, on earth, girls want to be friend after breakup? If they are so emotionally attached, then what was the need for the breakup?*

"Please, Riya. Let's not get into the depth. I know, why you broke up with me? Just to meet your dreams. Right? How could you be so selfish?"

"I know Arjun, you're hurt. But please listen to my version also. Don't I have the right to put my words?" Her voice choked.

*Gosh! Who in the world would be so cruel as to make a beautiful girl cry.*

"Say whatever you want to," I lowered my tone.

"You know my financial conditions very well. My father died, leaving a huge debt behind to repay. My mother was not a highly educated one, so she would do some little job to run home, and pay regular interest money. My mother was often harassed in front of people for not paying the debt money in time. Every time I saw my mother crying, I used to feel like kicking the ass of the person, who is responsible for all such trouble. Then, I decided, I will get back the dignity of my mother. I started working as a part time. I was focused to clear my exams and get a job to help my mom. During this time, I fell in love with you. At first, I liked you. But don't know how it got converted in real love. You're caring, loving, a perfect husband type guy, but I had something in my mind from beginning. I didn't want your family's help, because people will think I have used you as a weapon to pay off the loan. It will hurt my mom and my self-esteem. On the other hand, I found you to be too weak to take care of my ambition. So, I decided to part ways. I am really sorry Arjun. I know I have hurt you in many ways. But there were some reasons which made me take such a bold step. Even I miss you a lot. Your morning kiss, your stupid messages when I am angry with you. Could you please accept my apology, and accept me as your friend" She looked into my eyes?

"I might forgive you with span of time, but I would never be able to accept you as a friend. I always thought you to be my life partner. I may not be able to treat you as my friend," I choked.

"If you would have been there in my spot, what would you do?" She darted straight-forward question on me.

"At least, I would have never played with someone's true feelings," I left in an instance.

"Holy Shit, you landed the job!" Ankit seemed to be more excited than me.

We were having our evening tea at our favourite *adda*. It's always refreshing to have tea while gossiping.

"Yup, but the asshole put certain cards to play. I need to sign a bond of three years. If I don't, I lose the job"

"Freak man. That guy really seems to be a manipulator. What you said?" Vicky was too curious.

"He had given me some time to think and reply. I am really out. I am feeling this is a good option. But at the same time, will my family allow me to sign a bond for three years? Dad has given me a span of two years. If I say him about the bond of three years, he will never let me do the job. I feel I am in deep trouble" I was disheartened.

"Hmmm. I feel you should pray to God. He will certainly show you some way to get out of this situation" Satyam was really a nice guy, but I always felt he should have become a *Baba*. *Wait a minute, even that's also a good business. Earn crores, and pay nothing.*

"Satyam, he needs our help right now, not some *pravachan*" Ankit interfered.

"I know you're a non-believer. But put your faith this time. You will see positive result" Satyam defended.

"Guys, please cut it out. I'll see what to do. You guys say, what happened to your interviews?" I was trying to deviate them.

"I have made it in E&Y. I'll be working with offshore clients" Vicky's eyes twinkled.

"Wow, now apart from Indian girlfriends, our friend would be making some foreign girlfriends too" Ritz chuckled.

"What about you Ritz? How was your interview?" I was eager to know, what this dumbass has done.

"Nothing. I was miserable in both interviews. They went too personal about my family" He choked.

Ritz's father left his mom and married some whore. Ritz's mother took a lot of pain to brought him up. All of us were aware of this fact, but we never brought up this topic.

"Didn't you smack that asshole? If I would have been there, I would have surely kicked his butt so hard, that he would never dare to ask such a question to anybody" Ankit was furious.

All of us felt bad about the interviewer's behaviour. *People dig fun out of somebody's pain.*

"Screw the interviewer. Anyways, I feel I am not born to be a slave" Ritz changed the mood.

"So, what do you want to do? Open up a tea stall" I tried pulling his leg.

"I don't mind doing it, moron. But I have some other plans. I want to open up a CA Firm. It would give me satisfaction, and I will be my boss. Nobody would ever dare to dig into my past". I could clearly see a pain in his eyes. His eyes were moist. *He was crying from inside but still making all of us laugh. I realized I was not the only miserable child on this planet.*

"Hey, that's a good idea Ritz. I, too, will join you as a partner. At least, I would be saved from my dad's hypertension business. Moreover, every weekend, we could have drinks party"

"You guys' suck. How can you start this partnership firm without me, Ankit and Satyam?" Vicky gave a disgusted look.

"By the way, I forgot to tell you guys. I met Riya in the campus. She, too, secured a job in a private Bank," I casually told my gang about this.

"Are you nuts? Why did you talk to her? Please don't tell me, Riya wants you back," Ankit clearly seemed irritated by this.

"Nope. Instead, she shocked me. She revealed her past," I narrated the whole story of Riya.

"What are you saying? She did all these just for dignity? How can she be so insensitive to put her dignity ahead of her love?" It was the first time I saw Satyam's different *avatar*.

"I don't know what she felt. But now, there is no more Riya chapter in my life. Now, I just need to think about the job prospects," I said as I finished my tea.

"Yeah, whatever happens, it happens for good," Vicky said. For a moment, I felt that Vicky and Satyam had changed their souls.

"Whatever you decide, please remember, it's your life. Any wrong decision can lead you into trouble," Ankit paid the bill.

"Don't worry buddy. I am a Marwari boy. I will never make any decision, which results in loss," I took leave.

"Hi, Sunaina" I greeted her after seeing her online. It's been a long time since I spoke to her.

"Hey Arjun, how are you? How was your interview? Did you get the job?" I felt as if she was more excited than me.

"Yup, I got one. It's a real estate company. But they have put a condition on my joining" I narrated the whole interview story.

"Hahahahaha...I can't believe you're so dumb. How do you get the courage to tell the truth? Amazing buddy" I could sense she was still laughing hard.

"I don't know, but it feels really hard to tell a lie, no matter who he is. It came out in a second. Maybe, I was nervous. So, I didn't realize what I was saying" I tried to prove myself innocent.

"Oh, little boy, you're so sweet"

"You say, how is your life going?" I tried to divert her attention elsewhere as I didn't want her to dig more about my interview session.

"Life is going cool. Everyday learning new things about fashion. Tomorrow we will have an opportunity to visit a fashion show. It is about winter collection. You know, who is the chief guest?" She darted a question without any option. *Maybe she thought I have a good knowledge about fashion, poor girl.*

"No idea. Maybe some film star or some politician" I tried to escape.

"No dumb, he owns a fashion house. Mr. Aman Sethi, the new Managing Director of Fashion Universe. He joined the company three years ago. He is promoting young talents. I wish, I get an opportunity of internship in his company" She finally stopped.

"I heard his name first time. Anyways, I wish you all the best. May you achieve whatever you desire"

"Now you say, what you have decided? Will you be signing this bond of three years?" She came with straight-forward question, which I was trying hard to avoid.

"I am in two minds. I don't know which way I should go. My heart says go for it, but my brain says- Are you nuts? You want to be a bonded slave for three years? I am more tensed, if my dad asks me to leave job after two years, and join his business, what am I going to do? I am really confused. What you think, I should do?" I sought her advice.

"Whenever I am confused, I close my eyes, analyse the situation, and do whichever is more favourable to me" I felt this was the shortest *gyaan* anybody gave to me.

"Quite simple. But in my case, I am finding both the situation in equilibrium. I am unable to judge, which one is better – Job opportunity at Ajnara Constructions, or trying to get job in some other company?" I laid my confusion in simple terms.

"Do you think the company having a very good brand value? Sorry, I am bit weak in this subject."

"Yup it's one of the best brands in real estate segment. And if I work with this company, it might help me to improve my skill-set with regards to knowledge, communication, personality, etc. I have seen those chaps working with Ajnara Constructions. Their attitude speaks about their pride of working with Ajnara. And I would be getting an opportunity to work with Mr. Naveen, who is such a good manipulator. In short, it's a good brand to work with" I stopped.

"If you think it will do more value addition in your skill-set than any other, then what is there to think about? They are asking you to stay with them for three years minimum, and I feel it's not a long period.

Besides, think about the challenge which you will get there, to prove your worth," Sunaina was making sense.

"Hmmm. I think you have made a good point. I will think about it. Catch you later. Time for dinner"

"I hope my advice shall help you. Take care buddy, will see you tomorrow. Good night. Sweet dreams."

"Thanks, Sunaina. All the best for the fashion show"

"Dumbo, neither I am the designer, now the show-stopper. I am going there, just to learn something and make good contacts"

"Oh, you're quite smart. Networking, ahem," I tried to pull her legs.

"Mr. Arjun, it's time for you to go to dine. Pull my legs some other time. See you tomorrow."

"Okay, Sunaina. Hope you have a good time at Fashion show. See you tomorrow. Good night sweet dreams." I logged out.

I felt relaxed. After chatting with Sunaina, I realized I was feeling positive about the job opportunity. *Maybe she is an angel, sent to help me whenever I am in stress.*

# Chapter-7

"How was your interview?" Dad asked me, without even glaring at me.

"It was good" I tried to avoid the topic.

"Did you get an opportunity to prove your "worth"?" Dad stressed more on the word *worth*.

"Yeah, I got one, almost." I realised I put matches in the gasoline.

"What do you mean by almost? Are you trying to play smart with me, or saying you're on the verge of rejection? I am still saying, work with me. Be the boss, and the world will appreciate your choice. Don't waste your time for some penny amount of salary. You still have the time, think about it" Dad was self-obsessed.

"Dad, I know what choice I have made, and I can easily figure out the consequences of my failure" I was getting bold.

"Do whatever you want. God knows how you were born into a Marwari family, who doesn't have the knowledge to calculate the loss, or gain in life" Dad seemed to be disgusted after a long argument.

"I know the loss. I know the gain. You just forgot, besides being a Marwari guy, I am also a CA" I didn't know how I got the courage to say.

"Fine, do whatever you want. I won't interrupt anymore," Dad left the table.

*It was the first time that dad left the table like this. All the other members were looking at me like I had murdered someone. My mom was having tears in her eyes. Others were concentrating on the delicious Matar paneer.*

"Hello, Anu here, calling from Ajnara Construction. Am I speaking with Mr. Arjun?" the moment came for which I was nervous.

"Yeah, Arjun here" I tried to show some confidence.

"Mr. Naveen wants to see you by 11 at the office. He wants to have a discussion with you regarding the last-day interview. Can I fix your appointment with him at 11 am?" She was too polite.

"Sure, Anu ji" I was nervous.

"Ok, Mr. Arjun. Your appointment has been fixed at 11 am with Mr. Naveen. Please be on time. He hates unpunctuality," she disconnected the call, before even listening to my *bye.*

I was feeling weak. Although I knew I wanted to join this company, something from inside, was stopping me from taking the opportunity. *Maybe it was the three-year bond, or the pressure of working under the big brand name. I kept on motivating myself.*

By the time I got ready, it was already 9.30 am. I rushed to my scooty to avoid any further delay. By the time I reached Ajnara Constructions, it was 10.55 am. I thanked God for reaching on time, almost.

"May I come in, Sir?" I knocked on the cabin door.

"Come in" Mr. Naveen sounded severe.

I entered the cabin. It was like a 1 BHK house size. A designer table with matching designer chairs was in contrast to room paint. The colleen on the floor was looking beautiful. The cabin was on the 17$^{th}$ floor; I was able to see the Bangalore city ahead of Mr. Naveen's chair. The interiors seemed to be imported. The AC was running too chilled. But still, I felt, it was hot. *Maybe I was too nervous to face him again.*

"Good morning, Sir" I greeted.

"Good morning, Arjun. Until you accept my offer, you may call me Mr. Naveen," *I don't know what he was trying to do – sound modest, or professional.*

"As you say Mr. Naveen," I replied similarly.

"Getting back to the business, I wanted to discuss the interview session. I called you up to find out about your decision. I guess one night was enough to think about this golden opportunity. What's your decision?".

Before I could reply, his phone rang.

"Hey sweetheart, I will call you back in sometime. Right now, busy with some stuff" *I was figuring out, who was the stuff – me, or my selection.*

"Sorry, Arjun. Tell me your decision. If you're willing to accept our terms, the papers are ready" he says pulling out an e-cigarette.

"Sure Sir. I have made my decision, I am okay to sign the bond for three years," I was feeling proud. *Finally, I did it.*

"Great, Arjun. We will do the paperwork now. You may join from next week. Wish you all the best" He picked up his phone.

"Shweta, please come inside with the documents"

After a minute, a beauty entered the room. She was wearing a Western outfit. Her bosom was quite visible. *God knows, why girls wear such dresses at the office. Either way, a guy ends up being nervous.*

"Hello, Mr. Arjun. Could you please come with me, so we can finish our paperwork"?

"Uhhh...Oh sure," I could hear my paced-up heartbeats.

"Easy, Arjun. She is not going to eat you." Finally, I saw Mr. Naveen's other face - A witty one.

"Right, Sir. I'll take your leave" I was quick to leave the room.

"Hey, Sunaina, I accepted the offer," I have been excited since noon to tell her this news.

"Hey that's great. Well done, Mr. Arjun" She was equally happy for me.

"So, tell me, how was your fashion show? Did you make any contacts?" I was finding the topics to talk.

"Arjun, it was really hard to make any contacts. All the people were either busy gossiping about each other's lives over cocktails or planning the next-day event. To be frank, I felt it was a waste of six hours for me. Only one hour was productive. Some good designers were there. It was good to see the way they presented their collections," she said it all at once.

"So overall, you had a boring session 😁"

"Ha ha ha... yeah it was. By the way, it was a fake laugh. So, when are you joining there?"

"Next week. I wish things go in my favour"

"Arjun, can I say something, if you don't mind?" For the second time I saw her being so reserved.

"*Bindass*. Say anything you feel like," I was waiting, what she was going to say.

"Arjun, try to put faith in yourself. You are really good. You passed CA in a maiden attempt. You got a job in a big company. What makes you feel so low?" I never thought she would be so straightforward.

"I have faith in myself buddy, but I don't know why I feel so nervous when things come on me" I tried to explain to her.

"Try to face things, instead of running away from it" *I found a genius on the other side.*

"Yeah, I will do it" I tried to escape it, as usual.

"Sorry to bug you with my lecture. Going out for some work. See you later" I could sense, she was offended by my casualness.

"I am really sorry. I know you're hurt by my casualness. But this is the way I am" I tried to explain to her.

"Arjun, if we have some bad habit in us, we should try to fix it, rather than running away from it" she logged out.

*Was I really a loser or she was unhappy for making no contacts at the show, and blasted it on me? I felt, the second thought was more genuine.*

"That's great news buddy. We must celebrate it. Finally, you did what you wanted to" Ankit was too excited after hearing that I accepted the offer of Ajnara Constructions.

"Yeah man, it's a party time. Tonight, we can go to a disco" Vicky was always ahead in making those expensive ideas.

"Yeah, man. It's been a long time since I had gone to the disco. Let's try out the new disco in Whitefield" Ritz was in a full swinging mood.

"Guys, let's go to some decent restaurant, have dinner and come back home" *I am pretty sure you guys can make out who he was, our saint – Satyam.*

"Satyam, I have one request. If you don't have a better option, please shut it" Ritz was in no mood to try some *good restaurant.*

"Ok, guys let's not debate. My family is out for two days. We could have fun at my place. Moreover, last day my dad got a new home theatre system. Let's try it out with some great movies" Ankit finally made a pocket-friendly idea.

"I hope some decent movie. Not like the last time when you played a porn" Satyam looked worried.

"Ha ha ha...no no buddy. This time I will play some Hollywood flick for you guys" Ankit laughed.

"Ok, Bro. Plan done. We are coming to your place by 9:00 pm. Keep the stuff ready" Ritz sounded like a boss.

"Hey, asshole you're not a big daddy. Somebody needs to accompany me to buy the stuff" Ankit replied similarly.

"Arjun will accompany you. Moreover, he has good contact with Manali staff guy" Vicky winked at me.

"Fine. We will get these things. But don't be late" I finished my tea.

"OK done. See you guys at 9:00 pm at my place" Ankit too finished his last sip of tea.

"Get extra stuff of Manali. I might go beyond control tonight" Vicky replied while finishing his tea. *I guess Vicky was already in a drunken state.*

"Ok guys. We all will meet at 9 near Ankit's house".

All left leaving me and Ankit behind. The liquor supermarket was at 100 metre distance, but the stuff to carry was dangerous. So, we decided to take my car. We reached the store in no time. Ankit straight away headed for the beer section.

"Hey bud, can I talk to you for a moment?" I asked.

"Go ahead, dude. You don't need to take my permission" Ankit was figuring out which one to take.

"Do you really think I am a nervous kind of guy? A run-away-from tragic-situation guy?" I wanted to know whether Sunaina was right.

"Are you in your senses? What kind of question is this?" Ankit couldn't figure out what was wrong with me.

"I just want to know whether I am a nervous type guy or not?" I couldn't control my patience anymore.

"To be very frank, you lack self-confidence. You're a genius, but still, you doubt your ability. Many a times we have seen; Riya was wrong but still you evaded the situation with your casualness. It may hurt you in the long-term buddy. If possible, leave this habit of running away from the situation. I am sorry if I am hurting you, but as a friend, it's my duty to tell you the truth" Ankit was serious.

I was struggling to find some words in my defence, but all in vain. I found none. *Am I so weak?*

We finished our purchase, but my mind was still in the other world. *How can a girl, whom I met just some days ago, get to know so much in-depth about me? Was it Riya, who created a fake ID, just to make me overcome my issues, or was it really Sunaina, a girl from Mumbai, who never met me personally?*

"Hey, you OK?" somebody brought me into the real world. Ankit had paid the bill, and was waiting for me to take the lot from his hands.

"Oh, sorry buddy, I didn't realize you were done with the shopping" I took a lot from him.

"Don't be sorry. In fact, I am sorry. I shouldn't have said all such things. I guess it has affected you. Sorry buddy" Ankit tried to soothe me.

"No No buddy. Don't be sorry. I was living in some illusion that I was confident. I can do anything. But you brought me back into my senses. Lucky to have a truthful friend like you"

"Now let's move asshole. We need to find that Manali stuff too. By the way, why in the name of God you're asking me such a weird question? I never saw you talking about such topics. *Kisi ne kuch bola kya.* Don't tell me; Riya called you up, scolded, and you haven't replied to her back." Ankit gets furious as soon as Riya comes into the picture.

"No buddy, it's not Riya. I have one online friend, Sunaina. She is from Mumbai, doing her Fashion designing course. While chatting, she told me this. I didn't believe her. I was scared to ask it from others. So,

I thought to ask you. Please, it shouldn't come out" I pleaded.

"Hmmm... so again a girl. Good going. How long you have been chatting with her?" Ankit was interested in this, but I knew what mischief was going on, in his mind.

"Around 2-3 weeks, but I know what you're hinting for. So, please spare me the horror" I replied.

"Hmmm...I must say. The girl has got something. Just in 2-3 weeks, she got to know what kind of person you are. Riya took at least half a year to figure this out" *God knows what the hell is wrong with this guy. Why does he keeps bringing Riya into any topic?*

"Just forget it, dude. Let's get the weed from Shafique" I tried to divert his mind.

"See, you always run away from things" he winked at me playfully.

"You guys took such a long time. What were you doing guys?" Ritz blasted on us as soon we reached Ankit's home.

"Asshole, who asked you to come so early?" Ankit was finding his keys to open the door.

It was 8:30, and Ritz was there before schedule.

"I just came to see the Manali stuff. Thought of taking a test of it" Ritz giggled.

We entered the house. Ankit lit the lights of the room. We took out the stuff. Lots of Beer cans, One Bottle of tequila, and Manali stuff which I bought.

"Wow, tonight nobody will sleep" Ritz was excited as if he never witnessed such a quantum.

"Exactly, how do you think we are going to finish this stuff?" Ankit winked.

"So, what are you planning to do till next week" Ritz finally asked something sensible.

"No idea. Maybe I'll go on a vacation" I badly wanted a vacation.

"Great, even I also want a vacation. Let's go to Ladakh" Ankit chalked out the plan for vacation.

"No buddy, I am planning to go to Mumbai, to my maternal uncle's place" I replied.

"I know why you want to go to Mumbai?" Ankit chuckled. *The asshole can never keep his emotions down.*

"Why? Tell me why he wants to go to Mumbai?" Ritz was also excited.

"Our Arjun is seeing a girl on the internet. She is from Mumbai. Maybe our hero is in love, once again" Ankit laughed loudly.

"How come you know that he is seeing a girl in Mumbai?" Ritz was too much interested to know about girls.

"Our hero told me," He pointed his finger at me.

I was ready for the blow.

"You asshole, bloody shit, you have hidden this thing from me," Ritz was furious on me, for no reason.

"Why the hell you guys are diverting the topic? I have no plans to meet her. And why the hell she would like to meet a stranger, whom she knows for nothing" I put my defence.

"Maybe you're not having any plans to meet her now. But I am sure you will ask her to meet. And who said, she knows nothing about you" Ankit was a nasty asshole. *He knows how to trap a person in words, and grill him mercilessly.*

"Ok. The topic ends here. I want no more discussion. Let's call up the other folks, and open up the cans. I need some badly" I tried to escape.

"See. You have a bad habit, of leaving the things in the midst" Ankit was still pulling my legs.

"Enough. No more words on this topic, assholes" I had to raise my voice to stop the topic. *But within I was thinking – what would be her reply, if I asked her to meet?*

*Will she say 'yes' to meeting a stranger, or she will simply reject my request?*

A doorbell broke my thoughts. Other members of the gang came. Ankit went to receive them.

"Oh, great guys. A lot of beer and *Manali* stuff is there. I guess, nobody will be able to sleep" Vicky was overwhelmed.

"Yeah man. If someone tries to sleep, he will have a good time with others" Ankit all prepared for mischief.

Each of us took the chilled beer and played the music on the Boulder's home-theatre system. The music was high, and the booming sound was making us shake our legs.

"Amazing sound quality, buddy. When did you get this?" Vicky asked.

"On my birthday" Ankit was feeling proud.

"Oh OK Nice gift *yaar*" Vicky replied.

"Are we simply going to listening to the music, and drink beer, or shall we light the Manali stuff?" Ritz was too eager for Manali stuff.

"Wait asshole. First, enjoy the music. Don't worry, we have enough weeds for the whole night" Ankit ignored Ritz.

Frankly speaking, the music was making us go high. Justin Timberlake is a perfect choice when you want to get drunk, and stay in ecstasy. The whole dining area was vibrating as if they were also enjoying the music. The clarity of sound made the ambience more pleasant.

"Hey guys, Arjun is planning to visit Mumbai. Moreover, we all are, too, having no reason to stay in the city for a week till our jobs resume. I am also thinking of visiting Mumbai, what about you guys?" Ankit was more like an enemy than a friend.

"No Ankit. I am going out of town with my family. So, I won't be able to accompany you guys" Vicky brought some relief to me.

"With family? Where are you going?" All of us echoed together.

"Some religious place in Devgarh. Mom made some *mannat*, that if I clear my CA exams, she will visit Goddess Durga temple in Devgarh town" Vicky explained.

"Wow, that's nice. So, when are you leaving?" Saint Satyam was more excited.

"Day after tomorrow" Vicky took his sip.

"What about you two guys?" Ankit pointed towards Ritz and Satyam.

"I may go out with family in a function. Count me out" Satyam gulped his can down.

"I have got no job. So, I have to search for clients and need to apply for a Certificate of Practice at the earliest. So, I am really sorry guys" Ritz said. I was happy to hear this.

"Ok. So, now it's only me and you, to go to Mumbai" Ankit chuckled.

"No way. I am going to my maternal uncle's place. So, don't take it as some adventurous vacation" I was trying to avoid this issue.

"Aren't you going to meet Sunaina?" Once again, he narrated to everybody about Sunaina.

"Hey Arjun, I am ready to accompany you to Mumbai. I'll ask my mom to visit Devgarh some other time" Vicky joined Ankit.

"Yeah Arjun, even I'll drop the plan to attend the family function" Satyam also changed his tune.

*What the hell with these? Moment ago, all of them were making excuses on the pretext of some crap family vacation planning. And suddenly when they heard about Sunaina, all of them were ready to pack their bags for Mumbai. Gosh! Why guys are so kiddish?*

"Let's stop it here. I have no plans to meet her. Moreover, why a decent girl would like to meet a stranger?" I tried to defend myself.

"I know what you have in your mind, Arjun. Moreover, if a girl meets any stranger, it doesn't mean she is not a decent girl. Even our best friend, was once a stranger to us" Ankit always has his answers ready. *God! Why did you make him so witty?*

"Ankit is right. And I love meeting strangers, girls. That doesn't mean I am not decent" Vicky supported Ankit.

"What are you doing asshole?" Satyam shouted at me.

I realised that after Vicky finished his statement, I laughed out loudly, and puked the beer on Satyam. I was still unable to control my laugh.

"What's wrong with this asshole Arjun? Have I cracked any jokes? Don't you think I am decent," I realized Vicky was serious.

"No buddy, it's not like that. I just laughed on that stranger's topic," Somehow diplomacy helped me.

"I know asshole what you're trying to say. Even though I have multiple affairs, it doesn't make me cheapo guy, or indecent chap?" Vicky was really mad at me.

"Ok, I'll prepare the Manali stuff. Vicky, please come with me to help" thanks to Ankit who didn't let it to take an ugly turn.

"Arjun, please don't think that I am the wrong guy. I am not taking advantage of anybody's faith," Vicky got emotional.

"I am sorry buddy. I didn't mean it. I am really sorry if you're hurt," I apologized for no reason.

"It's OK" these two words relieved me.

"We all went towards the centre table, where Manali stuff was kept. Segregating task, as usual, was given to Vicky. He was good at it. Vicky was carefully picking up the stuff to puff.

"Now remove the tobacco from the cigarettes. I'll put this stuff into the cigarettes" Vicky was working professionally.

We removed the tobacco from the cigarettes, and Vicky put the puff stuff in the cigarettes. All of us grabbed our shares, and lit the cigarettes. After taking the first shot, I felt I got a hit. Mind was feeling relaxed, soul was resting. I checked every one. All of them were quiet, enjoying their shot. Maybe they were enjoying it as if it was an ecstasy.

"Life is so brutal. I wish I would have not cleared my CA exams" I was shocked to hear this statement. It was our saint. *Maybe the Manali stuff has taken over him.*

"Yeah man, even I feel the same. Now all of us would be busy in our work life. I guess this is the last time we are meeting like this" Vicky joined the league.

"Could you guys please come back to your senses?" Ankit interrupted in the sad mode. "Don't worry guys, even if our lives get busy, we will still be in touch. I don't know about you guys, but I am really blessed to have such a good set of friends". I felt there is something wrong with the Manali stuff. All of them were getting emotional except me.

"True man, even if I am busy in audits, I will take out the time to be with you guys" Ritz was the next to join the club. Suddenly, I felt All the eyes were gazing at me. Maybe they were thinking it's my turn to get emotional. "I wish we could meet like this even if our life gets busy" I took my puff.

"What's wrong with you? Is your mind disturbed?" Ankit was quick to notice it. But I tried not to bring it out.

"No buddy. I truly feel we must meet like this, as we are meeting now" *It's easy to avoid your girlfriend, but not your best friend.*

"Dude, I don't need to tell you how well I know you. You can share with us what's troubling you within. After all, friends are there to share...". "Only your emotions, not your girlfriends" Vicky interrupted.

Suddenly, the atmosphere changed. All of us were laughing at this. Then, Vicky changed the topic.

"So, how's the crowd in office?" I knew very well, what he was hinting for. "It's pretty good. A lot of good-looking chicks are there to divert your mind" I winked at him.

"Bro, do something. I also want to join this company," Vicky pleaded.

"Then get yourself screwed with his boss Naveen in the interview" All of them said in unison. We finished the stuff. By the time we got up from chit chat, it was 3 in the morning. We decided to call it off, and rest in peace for some time.

"I know buddy, something is troubling you. Is it Riya, or is it your new job?" Ankit darted his straight-forward question.

"None of them. It's just the memories of my past, which is hounding me," I switched off the lights.

# Chapter-8

Finally, the day arrived for which I had been waiting for ages, and it was my first day in the Office. I woke up with zeal. I checked my wall clock; it was just 5 in the morning. *Gosh! Your sleep fades away when you're excited.* I tried to go back to sleep, but I couldn't. To escape boredom, I thought of surfing on the net. As soon I signed in, I saw messages from Sunaina. She didn't forget about wishing me on my most precious day. I smiled and replied to her back with warm thanks. I realized I was fond of her. I love to chat with her, and talk to her for hours. Does she also feel the same?

Keeping aside my thoughts, I started surfing over the internet. I thought of watching porn. It's the best way to complete your morning chores. But I don't know; something stopped me from within. Suddenly, a message popped up.

"Hi Arjun" I was right to guess. It was Sunaina. *Sometimes, I feel God hears me very well.*

"Hi Sunaina, how are you?" I was trying to hide my expression.

"Good to see you're awake so early," Sunaina said.

"Yeah, excitement to go to the office didn't let me sleep," I winked at her.

"So, all set to attend your first day in office, Mr. Arjun?" Sunaina asked.

"Of course, I am. Quite excited to attend it" I replied.

"Good to hear this. For the first time, I heard you're not nervous" I took it as a compliment.

"What about you? You're awake so early?" I asked.

"Having a fever, so I wasn't able to sleep" she replied.

"Then, what the hell are you doing over here? Take some medicines, and go to sleep. You

shouldn't be chatting right now" I blasted on her for no reason.

"Easy Arjun. I know you consider me as a good friend, and care for me. But I can take care of myself very well" she replied in a nonsensical tone.

"Fine, then take care of yourself in your way. Bye," I disconnected the chat session without giving her a chance to say bye. *How rude I was.*

Anyway, I got up, and went to complete my daily chores. Finally, I was ready for my first day in the office. I looked into the mirror to see if something was missing. I found everything was perfect. I was wearing a dark blue shirt, with contrasting Black trouser. The shoes were neatly polished; hair was neatly combed. It was time to leave.

I took my scooty keys, and drove them to the Office. I checked the time. and I was pretty early to reach the office. After noting my details and checking my appointment letter, the guard let me in. I went to the Accounts section and found an empty room. I took my seat in a small chamber. Probably, it was a Small Conference room. I kept on waiting for hours. Colleagues started taking their respective seats. They were looking at me as if they were seeing a tiger in a cage.

Moments later, the damsel entered the room.

"Good morning, Mr. Arjun" Shweta greeted.

"Good morning, Madam" I was too professional.

"You may simply call me Shweta. We are colleagues, not employer-employee," she replied with a cute smile.

"Let's go. I will introduce you with your team members. Then, we will have a half-hour session for HR induction" she briefed me about the upcoming events.

"Sure, let's go," I replied with a smile.

"He is Mr. Suresh, an accounts executive who takes care of purchases and does works-contract accounting. He has been with the company for the past three years. And, Mr. Suresh, he is Mr. Arjun, who is joining as an

Assistant Manager in your department. He is a CA." She finished our introduction.

"Oh great, you're a CA" *I didn't know how to handle such an expression. Whether he doubted that I am a CA, or was he over-whelmed to have another CA in this office.*

"Yes, Suresh *ji*, I am a CA" I proudly said.

"Good to see you, sir. Hope to have a long association with you" his wording made me feel suspicious. *What he is trying to say? Am I going to be kicked out of the office very soon?*

"Let's move to another person Arjun," Shweta said.

"Hmm yeah"

"She is Mrs. Padmini, Accounts Senior executive. She has been associated with company from past 5 years. She takes care of Bank and cash related data entries and work. And he is Mr. Arjun, a newly hired CA for the post of Assistant Manager" she finished the introduction.

"Good to see you Sir. Wish you all the best" she greeted.

"Thanks, Padmini *ji*" I replied with a soft smile.

Shweta took me to another desk.

"He is Mr. Mani. He takes care of the Customer's collection. He has been with the company for the past 5 years. And, he is Mr. Arjun, a newly qualified CA. He is joining us as an Assistant Manager" she finished.

"Good Luck," Mani replied and got focused to the computer screen.

I found it very embarrassing. Since it was my first day, I couldn't say anything to him because I didn't want to make it ugly.

"Thanks Mani *ji*," I replied politely, and left to meet the other guy at the desk.

"Don't mind him. He behaves like this with everyone, sometimes, even with me" Shweta explained.

"Meet Mr. Atul; he takes care of the Finance activities of the company. And, he is Mr. Arjun, Assistant Manager for Accounts Dept." She was good in introducing people. Maybe it's her daily chore.

Finally, she took me into a cabin, which was, of course, smaller than Mr. Naveen's cabin, but it was well maintained. The furniture was classy. The carpet was very clean. The cabin had a wall of glass, beyond which one could see the rising sun. A geeky young guy, around 27-28 years was sitting with his laptop open.

"Mr. Sharath, Mr. Arjun is ready to join our company from today. Mr. Sharath is the manager of Accounts and Finance. He has been associated with the company for the past 4 years" She introduced us briefly.

"Nice to meet you Sharath," I extended my hand for greetings.

"I would be happy if you added sir after my name," he bluntly replied.

"Sure, Sir," I replied in a low tone.

Finally, Shweta took me to the monster, Mr. Naveen. I don't know why; my heartbeats were speedy and uncontrollable, like an F1 car on a track.

"Good morning, Arjun. From today, you're part of this prestigious organisation. I hope you will prove your worth to this company by giving your best" *Thankfully the speech was short and decent.*

"Sure Sir, I'll do it" I replied.

"Great. I'll ask the IT department to provide you with the laptop. In case you require anything else, you may speak to Shweta. In the next 15 minutes, Shweta will conduct an induction session, where you will be briefed about the company's history, its principles, values, and policies. I'll see you after lunch" Mr. Naveen completed his sentence without even looking at me for once.

I left his cabin with Shweta for induction. I was asked to sit in the conference room. The room was large, and so was the table. Looking at the seating arrangements, at least 15 people could be inducted at a time. At the end of the table there was a projector with a white board on its front. Wires were tangled correctly under

Colin. A speaker handset was kept at the center of the table.

Shweta entered the room with her laptop.

"Hi Arjun, let's begin the induction session". She connected her laptop with the projector, and started briefing me about the company's history and its promoters. All the time I was looking at her. I was noticing her very closely. Her lips were like a blooming flower. Her eyes were appealing. Her nose was sharp n amazing. She was dressed in a black skirt with a white shirt and a blazer on it. Her stilettos were giving her an additional height of around 3 inches.

"Arjun, are you clear with the policies of the company?" her voice shook me.

"Umm yeah, I got it" I guess she realized I wasn't taking note of whatever she was saying.

"I'll ask the IT personnel to give you a laptop. In case, you require any stationery items, you may ping me. In case you require any other assistance, you may call me on 127, or ping me on corporate chat room," she said in one breathe, as if it was by heart.

I came back to my seat. In a minute, a giant shadow appeared walking towards me. I looked up to see the demon. A guy with dusky skin complexion and a huge belly with a giant height of around 7 feet stopped at my work-station. Looking at his stature, my words froze down. I could barely speak, Yes Sir.

"Your laptop and other necessary accessories are here sir. Kindly sign this receipt of laptop letter," I took the letter, signed and returned it.

"In case you require any IT support or help, please feel free to call me at 144. My name is Krishna, have a nice day ahead sir" with this, the demon left my workstation.

I checked the laptop. It was configured with latest version of Windows OS. My workstation phone rang.

"Come into my cabin" the guy kept the phone. *God, these arrogant seniors don't have time enough to say their identities. It felt like he was paying for per-second calls.*

With my intuition, I went into Mr. Naveen's cabin. I knocked the door like a professional.

"May I come in, Sir?"

"Come in" without even looking who is there at the door.

"Sir, did you call me?" I asked.

"Yes, we have received some notice from the VAT Department. Sharath is taking care of it. I want you to get involved in this. You would be assisting Sharath in this matter. Work under his guidance, and try to finish it as early as possible. Some other important work is in queue for you. Have you got your laptop?" After a long speech, he pounded a question.

"Yes Sir, I have got it" I replied.

"Good, after lunch you will undergo the IT training. Since you're new to the IT environment we are using, I need you to undergo the IT training which is mandatory for all the employees. After completion, a test will be conducted to check your ability to handle the system" he stopped. *The last sentence infuriated me within. I was about to shout – dare you tell me about my ability to handle a system. I am working on such things when you might not know what a system is.*

"Sure sir, I'll do it," I sounded politely.

"Ok you may go now," He glances his eyes towards his system again.

I left his cabin, and moved towards Sharath's cabin.

The geek was glued to his system. I knocked on the door to ask his permission to enter his cabin. With his hands, he gave me clearance to land in his cabin.

"Naveen Sir told me to assist you in some VAT notice work. Could you please update me about the scenario?" I asked politely.

He gave a glance to me, and shook his head.

"I don't understand why Naveen put people on me without speaking to me?" He spoke out his frustration.

*People on your head. What the hell do you mean by it, you geeky cheesy fellow? At 27-28 years of age, you look like an uncle, and you're calling me a burden.*

"What happened, Sir?" I unintentionally said.

"Nothing. Have a seat. Here is the notice. Just read it. I will provide the supporting in mail," He handed me a piece of paper, and glued it back to the system.

I left the cabin. I saw the people at workstations. They were working like a machine. Without a pause, they were hitting the keyboard constantly. Nobody was talking to anybody. *At this point I wondered if I had I joined a company, or some military organization?*

I rested my bump on my workstation. The notice was about some default of payment by the company, for which company was asked to provide the documents and evidence in order support its calculation. People were getting up for lunch break. I, too, thought of taking a break.

"Hi, Arjun, looking for a company?" the eye-candy appeared.

"Hi, Shweta" I greeted her.

"Would you like to come with me for lunch?" She invited me smilingly.

"Yeah, I would love to. I am going out for lunch. Would you like to come with me?"

"Sure. Let's go out. Even I am also bored of eating regular food" she accepted my invitation.

"So, how is your day going? I guess quite boring" she cheekily asked.

"You may say so. I always imagined office life fun-filled, but my imagination is quite away from reality. People are so serious on their work-station. Even school kids are better than them. At least they seem to be energetic" I blasted my frustration without even thinking a once.

"Easy Arjun easy. I know you're bugged up, but since it's your first day in office. Give some time to it. You will feel good" she uttered while taking her bite.

"I hope so," I was in no mood to talk more about my first day in office.

"So, you have joined the company just to prove your worth? Quite interesting," I was surprised to hear this from her.

"How you know this?" I was trying hard to swallow my bite.

"Mr. Naveen told me. I am really impressed. Being so wealthy, and having a well-to-do family business, a guy is out here to work in someone else's shoes and prove his worth" she replied.

"Thanks, buddy"

"So, do you have a girlfriend?" I wasn't expecting her to ask it so suddenly.

"I am sorry for such question so sudden," she was quick to realize the situation.

"It's ok. At present, I am single. I had a girlfriend in past," I replied.

"So, what happened? Why did you guys break up? I am sorry for getting so personal. I asked it out of curiosity. If you don't want to share, it's ok," she said.

"It's ok" with that, I narrated my entire love story. I couldn't believe myself that I narrated my past to a person, whose surname also I don't know.

"OMG, how could she betray you for such a silly reason?" *I like it when a girl extends her sympathy when she comes to know how hard you were hit.*

"Anyways, leave about me. You tell about yourself. You have any boyfriend?" I asked.

"Why? You want to mingle with me?" she laughed out hard. *It's still hard to understand a girl's mind. When they ask you about your girlfriends, it was out of curiosity. And when a guy asks the same thing, they feel it's a flirting. Gosh!*

"Nothing like that. Just out of curiosity I asked" I replied.

"Nope, I don't have any" she took her last bite, & we left to attain the remaining day of our office.

◆

# Chapter – 9

"So, Mr. Hot Shot CA, how was your day?" was the first question Sunaina asked me after a disastrous day.

"It was good," Somehow, I tried to hide my frustration.

"I don't think so" Sunaina was right.

*How the hell does a woman gets to know whether the guy is lying or not. Do they have some sort of lie-detecting machine?*

"Yeah, you're right" with that, I puked out my frustration.

"Oh ho, So Mr. CA is now flirting with hot HR….hmmmm, going good dude ☺" now she knew how to pull my legs.

"Okay let's not go in the wrong direction. She is a nice girl, but I have no such intention" I was trying to guard myself.

"I know Mr. Smarty, what your intentions are! All boys are the same…hehehe," Sunaina said. *I was clueless about how to counter this.*

"Well, you say how your day was? How are your fashion design classes going?" I tried to divert her.

"It was good. Right now, we are getting free passes to exotic fashion shows. Yesterday, I had the chance to meet the famous fashion designer Rohit Batra. Oh my God, what a down-to-earth personality. He gave me some good tips about using colour combinations" she described her day.

"Good, so is he handsome?" I tried to give her the taste of her own medicine.

"The only thing I know is that he is very cute. And mister, don't try my formula upon me. It will never work" she answered smartly.

"Cool. So, how's everybody at home?" *It gets really hard to find a topic to talk about over a period of time, I realized it today.*

"Everybody's fine. How come you enquire about family today? You never asked about it earlier" *I was scared to give her the actual reason.*

"Nothing like that. I just thought of asking about them. Sorry if you felt fishy about it" I tried to throw some attitude on her.

"Don't mind it *yaar*. I am just kidding. Sometimes you really get pissed off easily," *she was perfectly right. How come a person knows so well the other in such a short span of time.*

"It's not like that. Anyways, chuck it. So, do you people get any outstation projects too?" I enquired.

"Choices would be there to attend a seminar conducted by our institute in other cities. Heard Bangalore has got the best review for a seminar," she replied.

"It would be great if you attend Bangalore seminar. At least we would get a chance to meet," I answered.

"Sure, but before that take permission from Shweta. Who knows she feel bad that her guy is meeting someone else 😜" She pulled my legs again.

"Don't worry about her. I'll keep her in dark about this. No worries 😜" I tried to return the flavour.

"Two timings huh. So bad dude" I couldn't control my laugh this time. *Yes, I have got her this time.*

"hahaha...you may say so. Hey I have to leave now. Hope to see you soon. Do inform me about your Bangalore trip. See you soon" I have already been called for dinner three times.

"Sure dude. I'll let you know. Keep in touch" she logged out.

*I told to myself, who said I am going to leave you!!!*

"So, how is your office life going?" Vicky asked me while we were sitting in my room & playing cards on a fine Sunday noon.

"Going good" I was aware of the danger coming towards me.

"Just good. We thought you'd be having the best time of your career" Ankit poked.

"I know where you guys are hinting. Shweta and I are just friends in and out of the office, so don't exaggerate the matter" I bluntly said.

"Don't lie dude. It's hard to believe that you're not interested in such a hot shot babe" Ritz exclaimed.

"Guys believe me. I have no feelings for her. She is just a good colleague in the office. That's it" I was trying hard to defend myself.

"Thank God. Since you're not interested in her, please introduce me to her" Vicky, as usual, came up with his *tharki* idea.

"No way, dude. She is a nice lady. And if she knows about your past, she might snap all her ties with me too" *Frankly speaking, I was not willing to snap my ties with her.*

"See guys. I told you. Our boy Arjun is now dating Shweta. Otherwise, why would he refuse to introduce me to her?" Vicky was in no mood to let go of this topic.

"Dude it's not like that. I really think she is a simple girl and she has no past like you have. Moreover, she is a good friend of mine. If you want, I'll introduce you to her, but you shouldn't lie her about anything. If you promise this to me, I shall arrange a meeting with her for you" I said.

Silence prevailed for a minute in the room as if somebody died.

"Dude, why are you so possessive about her? It's up to Vicky and Shweta how they take things. If you have something for her, you can share it with us" Ankit sounded correct.

"I don't know but I am sure I am not in love with her. She is a very decent and humble girl and I really don't want to hurt her or get her hurt because of me. Anyway, I'll ask her if she would like to meet Vicky. If she denies it, nobody will raise this question again" I sounded like a boss.

"Ok, if she denies, I will never force you on this topic again" Vicky gave his nod.

I took a sigh of relief. I was sure that Shweta would deny it. Suddenly, Ankit generated another storm for me.

"What about Sunaina? How is she? When is she coming to Bangalore?" As soon as Ankit finished his statement, the group stared at me as if I were a criminal, and it was now my turn to clarify.

"So, you think only Ankit is your friend, and not us? You didn't tell us that she is coming to Bangalore". I was always scared of Ritz' anger. This maniac has no control of what he says in anger.

"It's not like that, Ritz. Last night, we met for tea, and there, I told him that Sunaina has plans to come to Bangalore, but it's not final as of now" I tried to pacify the matter.

"Good, since now you have Sunaina, I can easily go with Shweta" Vicky winked at me.

"It's tough to find an asshole like you" I couldn't resist myself.

"And it's tough to find a guy who is so confused like you" Vicky took a dig.

*True, it's tough to find such friends who speak about your negative points on your face and not on your back. I was blessed.*

"So, tell us more about her? What does she do? What do you guys generally talk about?" Ritz seemed to be more curious.

"Nice and simple girl from Mumbai, doing a Fashion designing course. Her Father and brother are also CAs. She understands me very well. She is also an expert in leg-pulling, just like you guys. To sum it up, a simple decent girl with a good sense of humour" I still had more to say about her, but I prevented myself from doing so.

"Why on the Earth, it's only you who finds nice, decent girls? Every girl you met in your life, you found them decent. Riya was also one of them" Vicky realized his mistake the moment he completed his sentence.

"I am sorry dude. I didn't mean to hurt you. I am just saying that...." before he could finish, I interrupted.

"See I don't want to talk about this issue, especially about Riya. It was personal; it was my past. Please guys don't talk nonsense all the time. It may hurt someone's sentiments"

Realising the moment of heat, Ankit took over the charge.

"Hey guys, stop being so childish. And how come it became a personal issue to you, when all of us are involved in it? No more discussion on it" he was quite good at sorting out the issues.

"Hey "personal" boy, it's your turn. Play your cards" Ritz said, diverting us back to the game.

"So, how was your Sunday?" Shweta asked while taking her bite. It was a routine for us to go out for lunch.

"Quite good. Had a good time with friends, played cards, then went out for dinner" I described while having my bite.

"Oh great. I have heard Marwaris are excellent in playing cards".

"How was your Sunday?" I was waiting to hear something different.

"It was the usual routine. I completed daily chores, then did some office-related work, and then went to the pub with friends" *I already knew it.*

"So, how many girls stay in your PG along with you?" I enquired.

"First of all, it's not a PG. We have taken a flat on rent, and the expenses are shared by all of us. And secondly, why are you bothered to know about the other girls?" she winked at me.

"I Just...I...I simply asked it. Don't take it in other sense. I have no such intentions" I said.

"What intentions Mr. Arjun? May I know your wicked intentions" *I knew she has got the bell, and she will ring it the whole day.*

"Nothing, Miss Shweta. By the way, one of my friends wants to meet you" *Thanks to Vicky who helped me out.*

"Me? Why? What's the matter? And how come your friends know about me?" *I had to answer that silly question.*

"Obviously, it was me who told them about you. After hearing about you, one of my friends wanted to meet you" I finished my lunch.

"No dear. Right now, I am not thinking about relationships. I am happy to be single" Shweta was still having her food.

"Hey Hey put a brake. He is also not a guy for relationships. He just wanted to meet you, casually. Don't expect much" I winked.

"What do you mean by 'not a guy for a relationship'? What are you hinting?" Shweta asked me directly.

"I mean...I mean he is a guy who doesn't believe in a relationship" I didn't want to ruin Vicky's chance for date.

"Ok. I'll think about it. But tell him not to keep too much of expectations" she finished her lunch, and we got up for our walk to the office.

"May I ask you something?" I asked while walking.

"Don't be so formal at outside. We are friends outside the office. So, keep your ethics codes in your pocket" she replied.

"You said you don't want to be there in a relationship at this point. May I know what's the reason?" I asked.

She stopped walking and looked at me. Her eyes became moist, but she controlled.

"Arjun, there are always something in people's past which they don't want to bring out. Don't ask this again. I am sorry if I was rude, but I am very reserved on this issue" she started moving on. *She was yet to move on in life.*

"I am sorry. I ..I just asked casually. I hope you won't mind" I apologised.

"It's ok dude. Now let's go to office, else we'll get jacked" she said smiling.

◆

# Chapter – 10

Life was going smoothly. After a month or so, Shweta agreed to meet Vicky. Vicky came to my place half an hour before the scheduled time.

"What's the matter dude? I never saw you so tense. You are early by half an hour" I teasingly said.

"I don't know. Even I am surprised, why am I so nervous? It's not the first time that I am going on a blind date, but still I have no clue why I am so nervous" I was unable to hold my laugh on this.

"Shut up, you asshole. You're not understanding how much nervous I am," He finally took his seat.

"Easy boy. She is a nice lady. Don't worry at all. Just be yourself" I advised.

"Thanks. Keep your advice to yourself. If I believe your advice, it shall be my last date"

"Dude, trust me. Once you meet her, you will not feel nervous" I tried to calm him down.

"Yeah, let's hope for the best. Let's go. I don't want to be late" Vicky hurriedly got up, and we left for the venue to meet Shweta.

"Hi Shweta" as usual, she was late by 15 minutes.

"Hi Arjun. Sorry for being late" she apologised.

"Don't be sorry. We were prepared for it" I winked at her.

"Good" with a smile she turned towards Vicky.

"Hi, I am Shweta. And I am really sorry for being late" she said.

"It's ok. Never mind. I am Vikram". Vicky gracefully shook her hand.

"Ok birdies. I'll make my way out. You guys enjoy" I got up to leave.

"Where are you going? Have you also got one for a date?" Shweta asked cheekily.

"Not yet. But if I sit with you guys, I'll never find the one to date" I winked.

"At least be with us for 5-10 minutes. Then you may make your way" This time, I had to accept her request.

"So, Vikram, tell me something about yourself?" Shweta asked.

"Well, just like Arjun, I am also a CA, working with an international audit firm as a senior audit exec. I and Arjun are childhood buddies"

*Seriously, how this guy get the girl for a date. He was so nervous.*

"Dear, I know all these things. Arjun told me about this. Since Arjun knew you well, so I agreed to meet you" Shweta told smilingly.

"To be very frank, Shweta, I am mesmerized by your beauty, and I am unable to take my eyes off from your eyes. And because of this, I am unable to speak anything. I know, such cheesy lines you have heard many a times in your life, but this is the first time I am saying them to any girl" Vicky finished.

*Now I know how he gets a girl for a date. Bloody cheesy guy!*

"Oh really. So, it's the first time you're dating a beautiful girl" Shweta teased.

*Now I got to know why she was single till this date!*

"You may say so. It's the first time I am dating such a beautiful girl" Vicky was trying to hide behind the shield.

"Ok. Now let's get deeper into it. Beautiful or hot?" Shweta was really screwing the guy hard. I was unable to control my laugh.

"You have a hot figure, and a beautiful face" Vicky finally had the courage to say it up. *And he was right. I agree with him fully.*

It was time to blush for Shweta. We all laughed at this.

"So, Shweta, you tell me something about yourself!" Vicky asked.

"Well, I guess Arjun must have told you something about me. To put it simple, I am a straight-forward girl full of emotions. I like travelling and partying with friends. Since I am an independent girl, I don't prefer anyone interfering in my matters. I aim high for my career. And I don't believe in relationships at all" she said it all in one breathe.

I and Vicky were looking at her with no emotions on our faces. It was the first time I was hearing the other side of her. Realizing our situation, she broke the ice.

"Guys what happened? Are you ok?" She brought us back to our senses.

"Absolutely. I was expecting you will add some more to your description" A laughter busted.

"OK guys. I shall leave now. You people continue. I hope you guys enjoy the company of each other" With that, I lifted my bum from the seat and left.

"How was the date?" I straight away asked Shweta when we met in the office elevator.

"I am sure Vikram would have told you what happened after you left?" she had a devilish smile.

"I couldn't get in touch with him last day, that's why I am asking you. How was it? Was he decent with you all the time?" I said.

"Easy Easy, dude. You're asking me as if you have some fixed remuneration for setting me with him"

Realizing her statement, she went on correcting it.

"I am sorry. I didn't mean it literally. I was kidding. Please don't mind. I had a good time with him. Earlier, he was sounding nervous, maybe because you were around. But after you left, he was very comfortable and easy-going. It was good to meet a stranger like this for the first time" We reached our workstations.

"Great. Seems you guys had great company" I smiled at her.

"Let's get back to work Arjun. Mr. Naveen would come at any point of time"

"Hey, how are you? It's been a long time since I've seen you" I pinged Sunaina.

"Yeah, was busy with assignments. You say, what's new running at your end? Howz ur bombshell HR 😬 "

"She is good. Last day, she met Vicky. I guess they liked each other" I informed her about the happenings.

"Oh Great. So, you're single once again...hehehe 😆 " Sunaina was on her track to pull my legs.

"Yeah, you see how harsh my luck is ☹"

"Hehehehe...it's always a pleasure to chat with you. You know, I have many male friends, but none of them is as cool as you are" I was trying to figure out what she meant.

"Thanx mam ☺..It's all my pleasure"

"Arjun, I never asked you if you're dating any girl. I thought you may not like it, but I am curious to know if there is any lucky girl in your life"

It took me almost a minute to digest her question. I didn't know how this question came in the middle, and that too in such a weird way.

"It's ok if you're not comfortable to share it"

"It's not like that. I was surprised you asked me this question out of nowhere. Fine, I'll tell you. You might remember that when we chatted for the first time, you asked me about my campus plans and choice of companies. I told you that I hadn't planned anything since I was disturbed. The reason was my break-up. Her name was Riya" I told her everything in detail.

"I am so sorry to hear about that. I always teased you with other girls, thinking you're a shy fellow, but I never knew you had so much of a burden on your heart. I am really very sorry"

"Please, Sunaina, in fact, I am thankful to you for helping me out in my stressful time. When I met you for the first time, for a while, I forgot about Riya and our break-up. You have always been nice to me. So, please don't be sorry☺"

"Thanks Arjun ☺"

"Now let's stop this game of sorry and thanks. You say, you had any past?"

It was a long pause. My heart skipped a beat. I felt she also suffered the same brunt in her life. I was waiting for her to reply.

"I will tell you when I meet you next. I have to leave now. Mom is calling. See you later. Take care, have fun dear" She logged out.

*I was trying to figure out – Did she had a break-up too?*

"Hi busy boy" a sweet voice came from the other side. I knew who it was. It was Sunaina.

Recently, we exchanged our numbers and it was the first time she called me up.

"Hi dear, how are you?" I sounded husky, since I just woke up.

"I am good, what about you?

"I am doing good too. By the way, as I expected, you have a good voice"

"Stop flirting dude. I know how sweeeeeeeeeeeeeeeet my voice is."

"I am serious *yaar*. You really have a sweet voice. So, how's your Fashion course going on? How's everybody at your place?"

"Classes going great. Everybody is fine at my place. What about your side?"

"My life is going cool. Now well-settled in office. Things are also normal at home."

"You know, last day I was thinking and asking myself..." Before she could finish, I interrupted.

"What you were thinking?"

"It's just six months, and I have shared my number with a guy whom I never met. If you don't mind, can I see a picture of yours?"

"Nope, you can't. You can see me only when you visit Bangalore."

"Arjun, this is not fair. I know you're not so handsome, but it doesn't mean you can't share your pic" and a laughter busted after that.

I don't know why, but somewhere, I was feeling good to hear her laughter.

"Just kidding. I know you're a handsome dude and one of your colleagues has a crush on you. By the way, how is Shweta?"

"She is good."

"No Dumbo, I am asking how she looks like."

"Too good, a voluptuous figure with assets in proportion."

"*Chii*, so cheap. Never knew you could talk like that, huh?"

"Hahahahahahahaha...I was kidding. All the times you pull my leg, I thought to do something different today."

"Hmmmm... Okay, listen. I have to go now. I will talk to you later, and take care, dear," she said, hanging up the call.

I always felt nice, but today I was feeling very different. I don't know what it was, but I was really very happy after talking to her. *Am I in love? Can love happen twice? How can I love her, I haven't seen her yet?* My mind was full of such questions.

Days were passing normally. I successfully completed the span of 06 months in my office. People became friendly with me. Finally, the thing that I dreamt of was coming true. My performance was evaluated, and it was on the better side in each aspect. My colleagues were getting lighter with me. All of them turned out to be nice fellows.

Meanwhile, Vicky and Shweta became good friends. Ritz was getting settled in his practice business. Ankit & Satyam were also enjoying their job lives. Overall, all of us were having a good time. But as we all know; good time lasts only for a while. The same happened with me.

It was bright Sunday morning. I got up as usual in the latter half of the morning. After finishing my chores, I went to have my breakfast. I overheard my aunts talking about some girl.

A bad thought came to my mind instantly – *Is it a marriage proposal for me?*

I tried to find out the details and learned that the family was planning my marriage. Later, I learned about the girl. It was Shruti.

I couldn't believe it. *How come such great innovative ideas strike my family out of nowhere? Why they are so weird?*

"Mom, what is this? All of you are trying to get me hitched with Shruti? We are just good friends, why do you all want to take it further level?" I couldn't control my anxiety.

"Why, what's wrong with Shruti? She is good-looking, well-cultured, educated like you. Above all, she belongs to our caste, and we have known the family for a very long-time. Moreover, you and Shruti are close to each other, so there shall not be any problem?"

*Whether it be a movie or reality, the caste effect will always be there in Indian marriages.*

"But mom..." Before I could finish, I heard a heavy and husky voice from behind. It was Dad.

"See, this is the problem with our education system. Just because they can spell a few words in English, they feel they have more knowledge about worldly affairs than their parents." I just forgot to tell you; even education is *blamed if you are trying to put something different in front of your parents.*

"Dad, I am not saying like that. I am just saying...." I was obstructed again. This time, my aunt.

"Arjun, shruti is really a nice girl. Moreover, you know na, what kind of girls are there in our society? Like Riya, there are many others waiting for a big chunk of money. Even their character is also doubtful".

"But Aunty, just because of one girl, you can't blame others in society. There are other girls in society who are decent, well-behaved, well-cultured like Shruti." I realised I had *axed my own foot.*

"Now you got it right son. That's why we are talking about shruti for you" I can see a big smile on Aunt's face.

"Right now, I have no such intentions. If there is something, I'll let you guys know about it" With this, I left the arena quickly.

# Chapter – 11

"Hi Shruti, did you get the news about what's cooking between our families?" I was anxious to know what she was thinking.

"Yup, I got a call from Mom last night. I just laughed and laughed and laughed. My roomies thought I had gone crazy." I could still hear the sound of her laugh, though it was light.

"What's there to laugh? I am smart, handsome, and well-educated. Don't you think I can get any girl I want?" I popped the question.

"No No, I don't mean that. I mean I know you're already in love with Riya, so...." I had to interrupt.

"We broke up more than 6 months ago" I took a long breath after that.

"What the......? Are you serious? If it's a joke, I can tell you it's the worst one you can crack." Shruti couldn't believe what she heard, so I had to narrate the whole incident to her.

"I am so sorry. I didn't know about this. But how could you let her go? I mean, I have seen how serious you were about her." Shruti was trying to find an answer to her curiosity.

"Sometimes life takes you to the road which looks beautiful and you see a bright future from there. But suddenly, life takes a turn, and your dreams shatter. For Riya, her dreams were more important than my love. Anyway, I don't want to talk about it. I want to speak to you about something. I met a girl on Yahoo Messenger while chatting. Her name is Sunaina. She is a student of Fashion design. Recently, we exchanged our numbers. You know, she helped me unknowingly to come out from the sorrow of break-up with Riya" I said in a hurry.

"Easy Mr. Arjun. Calm down, dude. You seem to be in a hurry." I knew she was pulling my legs.

"Yeah, I am because I have to go to my office. I hope to catch you soon." I was about to hang up the call.

"Sure, Mr. Arjun. I will catch you soon to learn more about Sunaina. Till then have fun. See you soon, dear." She hangs up the call.

I took a deep breath, but I was still surprised. *How come I shared about Sunaina with Shruti so easily?*

"Congrats, dude, heard you're getting hitched," Ankit jumped on my bed.

"You're such an asshole. The news which we should get from you, we got it from someone else. What's her name by the way?" Vicky rested his ass on the bean bag.

"Have you guys lost it? Who said I am getting hitched?" I was surprised at how they learned the half-baked news.

"Sorry, we can't tell you the source. But your expressions prove that it's confirmed news." Ritz was good at maintaining suspense.

"Guys, it's a misunderstanding. Mom probably told to Ankit that I was getting hitched. Her name is Shruti, and we are childhood friends. Neither I nor Shruti are serious about this. So please don't fancy about it." I was trying to divert them.

"OH! So the girl's name is Shruti. Nice name by the way. What did she do?" Ritz was a case of curiosity.

"She is in London, doing her MBA. Now stop your How-I-met-my-wife show"

"Nice dude. Then, what's the problem? I always had a dream to study abroad" Vicky's eyes were wide-opened after hearing the *London*.

*God blessed those countries that didn't approve visa applications of Vicky.*

"Can we talk about something else? How is your dating going on with Shweta?" I turned the face of the missile towards Vicky.

"It's Going well. She is very decent, jolly, and frank by nature. I'm having a good time with her. Thanks a lot for getting me in touch with her." *Hearing Vicky make these sorts of statements, one can easily make out he has yet to get what he wants.*

"Dude, don't try anything wrong with her. You both are close and dear friends of mine. So don't ever put me in a tragic position" I warned Vicky.

"Don't be afraid. Even I don't want to try out anything wrong with her. I want to take this relationship for a long run. Let's see where destiny takes us" *I couldn't believe what I heard.*

"Congrats, dude, so you're also planning to be a family man," Ankit pinched Vicky.

"As I said, let's see where destiny takes us." Vicky suppressed the matter.

"Guys, let's make a move, or else we'll be late for our movie show" I reminded them about the movie plan.

"Hi Sunaina, what's up?" I was waiting for her sweet voice.

"Hey, I am good, how are you?"

"I am good. How is life going?"

"Going cool. You tell Mr. Hot Shot dude, how are you? Found any girl for romance?" *My heart skipped the beat. I wanted to tell her, yeah, it found one, and she has the sweetest voice in this world.*

"No dear. You're not here, so no romance. Hehehehe"

"Uh huh, so Mr. Arjun also knows how to flirt. Not bad. Going well, hopefully, you'll find one soon"

"You say you found anyone?" *I was waiting to hear a negative response.*

"Yeah, I have found one" *I never expected this reply.*

"I am talking to him over the phone right now, hee-hee" *Gosh! Sometimes, girls take your life away.*

"Oh, really babe. I am so glad you chose me"

"Oh, please, don't take it seriously. You're my best friend. Don't go into your imagination world."

"Hmmm"

"Hey listen; I shall be visiting Bangalore after 4 months. I had to choose a location for project, so I chose Bangalore. Will you guide me about the city when I come there?" *I couldn't ask for more. Thanks God. That is probably the second time I have said it.*

"Of course, you don't need to worry about anything. I will arrange everything for you." In my heart, the countdown started: *2928 hours to go.*

"Thanks a ton, dear. But I have a condition. We won't share each other's pictures. I want to meet you face-to-face"

*I was perplexed. Why did she not want to share a picture? How would we recognize each other?*

"But how will we recognize each other?"

"I don't know about you, but I'll definitely recognize you. Hey, listen I have to go now. I'm getting late for my classes. Will see you in the evening" *I can make out that she was in haste.*

"Sure dear, I'll see you soon. Take care, bye" I disconnected the call.

*I was really happy, but scared at the same time – what if she is not serious about me!*

"Arjun, I have some interesting work for you," Mr. Naveen informed me. *I knew something harsh was coming down the way.*

"Sure, Sir, I would love to take up that interesting job." *Employees like us have to speak like this to maintain the code of conduct.*

"Our half-year has ended. I want you to work under the guidance of Sharath. You have to close the books of accounts for half a year and prepare financials accordingly for budgeting purposes. You have the time of 14 days from today. In case you find any trouble, contact me or Sharath ASAP. I don't want any negligence in this matter." He signaled me to go out of his cabin.

*It was the first time I had mixed feelings after coming out from Mr. Naveen's cabin. I always wanted a task where I could play with numbers. Meanwhile, I had to work with Sharath who was a geeky ass. Moreover, the period given was very short. I prayed to God to help me out.*

"May I come in, Sharath, Sir?" I knocked on the door, as per etiquette.

"Come in, Arjun" As usual, he was glued to his system.

"Naveen Sir asked me to close the books of accounts under your guidance. I wanted to understand the course of action. How shall we plan to move ahead?"

"How much time has he allotted?" His expressions were saying he knew the answer.

"14 days"

"Ask him to prepare the financials by himself. Is it a joke? I shall be the only person who'll be running around the people for data, and he wants it in just 14 days." *For the first, I saw a geek turning into a demon. He loaded his gun and kept on my shoulder to open fire on Naveen.*

"Why do you think you're alone? I have seen the closing for the financial year. I'll do the task you assign. Don't underestimate me." I couldn't bear his tantrums anymore.

"Oh, so now a young kid has a voice with six months of work experience. If you have so much attitude, then do this task all your own," the geek challenged me.

*Although I knew how to prepare the financials from the finalized trial balance, I never did the finalization of accounts. It was a dicey position for me. If I accept his challenge, he'll put all his responsibility on me, which would be burdensome. If I don't, it will hurt my dignity.*

"It's not like that, Sharath. I'm saying that if I work with you, I'll get more exposure towards finalising books. And it will help you in the long run." I played my cards.

"How?" Now I knew I had got him.

"If I learn this task, you'll not be troubled from the next time. Mr. Naveen would directly hand-over this task to me. So, technically, this financial headache will be shifted to me" *I played my googly.*

"Ok, so you want to take me down in Mr. Naveen's eyes" *I guess he understood what I wanted.*

"No, Sharath. As I said, I'll be helping you in this way by sharing your workload. If you don't want me to share your responsibility, it's totally cool with me."

"Hmmm...Oh, okay, Arjun. Let's do it. But this is the first and last time I'll be helping you out on a book-closing task." *I was glad to tap down the geek.*

"Sure Sharath. Now tell me, what aspect do I need to take care of? What shall be my scope of work?"

"As I said, I am going to help you on this for the last time. It definitely means you're going to do all the tasks, and I'll be guiding you." *I was pinned down.*

"Oh, okay, sure, Sharath." With a half-hearted response, I looked at his face.

"First of all, get all the entries closed by the day after tomorrow. Ask all the executives to do their entries within a day or two. First, complete this task, then I'll let you do the other task." I moved out of his cabin.

I knew what was going to happen next. *I was about to drop an atom bomb on accounts execs, and I knew the reaction and consequences for that.*

"Arjun, please don't joke at the time of work. Do you think it is possible to pass all the pending entries in just one day?" Padmini was the first to react.

"I know it's not possible, but if we coordinate properly and help each other, we can do it. I know I'm asking too much, but we have to finish it on time. Management has a lot of expectations from us, and we shouldn't fail their expectations," I tried to convince them.

"We can understand that, but you also need to understand that it's not a small task. It would take a minimum of 5-7 days to complete all those entries, and you're asking us to clear it in just 2 days. You're asking too much." Suresh supported Padmini's worry.

"I can understand, but this is where we have to show our strength against all the odds. I can assure you that if we combine our efforts, we can achieve this target. Let's help each other. We have a wonderful chance to show management that when it comes to dedication, the accounts department is no longer behind the others." *Somewhere from inside, I felt as if I were contesting an election and asking people to vote for me.*

"We cannot assure you, Arjun, but we'll try to achieve what you want." *Somewhere, I found it to be negative.*

"Why did you take such an idiotic assignment?" I couldn't believe what I just heard from Shweta.

"What do you mean, Shweta? It's my job. I am paid for maintaining accounts of the company"

"I know it's your job. But did you try to figure out why you have been chosen for this work?" *I had no clue.*

"Sharath is responsible for presenting financials to the company. And Sharath was jealous of you since Mr. Naveen was giving weightage to you than him. Just to get you down in his eyes, Sharath played the trick and pasted the work on your head. He knows very well that these executive people will not cooperate to complete this task. I hope now you understand why I said so," I said to myself; *now I should also watch saas-bahu serials to understand politics better.*

"If it is so, then I would complete this task. Thanks for your help. By the way, how's it going between you and Vicky?"

"It's going well. He seems to be a nice guy. But sometimes I feel awkward."

"Why? What happened? Did he do something wrong to you?" I munch my bite.

"Nothing dude. Leave it buddy. It's my mistake. I'll take care of it."

"You both are my close buddies, and I can't see any one of you hurt."

"Last time when we met for a movie, he tried to smooch. But I was not comfortable. It's not that I never smooched a guy, but I don't know, I felt very uncomfortable."

"So what? You could have asked him not to do it."

"I didn't need to say it. He understood my problem and let it go. I need to take life easy."

"What burden you're having in your life?"

"Nothing dude. Work pressure and other stuff. Let's get back to the office. Our lunch hour is over officially." She took her last bite, and we left.

"Hey dude, what's up?" It was Sunaina.

"Hi dear, how are you?"

"I am good. What you doing?"

"I am good. How was your day?"

"Day was fine, very hectic. I have to meet my target in just two days. I don't know how to make it?" I narrated the whole incident to her.

"Don't worry about it dear. I have faith in your abilities. You can do it." *A thought crossed my mind – my dad sees me every day, but still, he doesn't have faith in me. She never saw me, still have faith in me. Amazing!*

"Thanks dear. Now I too feel I can do it" *Although I knew how tough it was to convince guys of age 35-40 to do work beyond their capacity.*

"You say dear, how was your day?"

"Mine was good. We are having a good time. All of us are excited to attend the Fashion shows and meet the designer and models in our assignment" I could sense she was eager to visit Bangalore.

"So what are there in your priority list when you visit Bangalore?"

"Many a things are there. Heard some expensive mall is there, where people like us just visit as if it's a museum"

*I knew she was talking about UB City Mall.*

"Definitely not dear. It's a place where you can get the most authentic and sophisticated things to gift someone special"

"Hahahahaha...Ok then I'll shop with you" I could sense she was trying to suppress her smile as hard she can.

"I hope to meet you when you come to Bangalore" I tried to find out whether she was interested to meet me, or she is trying to keep me happy.

"What hoping? Listen dude, I am coming there because I have the best buddy over there. Don't keep any other plans. I want to meet you and that's final. Complete all your pending tasks or assignments or whatever you call. I want to meet you and I'll take no excuses for it"

*Now I needed no further confirmation.*

"Oh okay dear. Just provide me with your itinerary details before your visit"

"Don't worry. Else I'll find you on my own. The most handsome, dashing, smarty...."

"Stop, you have added too many adjectives" We laughed out loud.

"Hmmm... No issues dude, for me you're a sweetheart. Now I need to go. Mummy is calling. Hope to catch you soon. Take care dear"

"You too, take care dear. Love you" *Unknowingly it came.*

"I love you too dear" *next I could hear was the sound of buzzing. I was feeling happy for what I just heard. But as usual, my mind took a negative route. Does she really love me, or she say it casually??????? Oh, I am so confused.*

◆

# Chapter – 12

The next day, I knew, was going to be the worst and hectic day. It was our last day to meet our deadlines for completing all pending entries. I came early to the office. I saw the quantum. It was a task for 2 days if we worked hard and a task for a week if we worked in a normal, casual way. I started working on one of the files. In a span of 15 minutes, I saw all the members of the accounts department were in the office. I was surprised to see their dedication. Now I know one thing: we are surely going to meet our deadlines. Each one of us took a file and started passing entries. I realized how important it is to work as a team when your neck is stuck in a bottle.

"Arjun, we have to get one more person to do this task, or else it will be difficult to continue. One of us also needs to take care of daily transactions" Padmini had the point.

"Who else can pass entries? Sharath?" I put an option.

"Don't even think of it. He's a jerk. A highly egoistic fellow whom this company is bearing," Atul warned me.

"But we don't have an option. One of us needs to be present to tackle day-to-day business. If all of us engage ourselves in this work, how we will meet our deadline?" I asked for opinion.

"Shall we seek the help of Murali?" Padmini gave an absurd idea, *according to me*.

"Madam, he is our office boy. How could he pass the entries? Do he even know how to operate SAP?" I controlled my anger.

"Arjun, he may be an office boy, but he works really well on SAP. We have seen it earlier. He used to sit with us to pass entries. I am sure, he could be a great resource" Padmini sounded logical.

"Ok, for a second, we accept he could help us. But there will be office work too, and if Mr. Naveen comes to know what he is doing, it could be dangerous for us" Atul comes out with a really scary thought.

"No worries, we can deal with it. After Murali finishes his daily chores, we can get him on the system" I suggested.

"Ok, but he would need a system ID and password. Who would be giving it?" Atul, although talking negative but making sense.

"Well Shweta can fix it for us" I was almost taken by shock with Padmini's idea.

"How? And how come she has got anything to do with accounts? She is already busy her payroll work" I tried not to involve Shweta in this mess.

"I know Arjun, Shweta is a very dear friend to you. But I am suggesting, she could give requisition for an additional laptop required to Krishna"

"The requisition can be sent by Accounts team too. Can't it be?" I countered.

"We can do it, but a good-looking girl gets things done easily rather than a sophisticated guy" Atul said.

"Ok I'll speak to Shweta and get us help" I left to meet Shweta.

I could see her, struggling hard with her payroll work. I knocked the door.

"Arjun, please don't bother yourself. You may come in" She welcomed me.

"Not like that. Someone told me it's about manners that you need to knock the door before you enter their place. You never know, they might be in an awkward position" I winked at her and we busted into a laugh riot.

"I need a small favour from you" I came directly on topic.

"You're always in a hurry. Tell me, how may I help you?" Shweta said.

"I need you to get me a laptop from Krishna with SAP for accounts installed on it"

"It's really tough. He would ask several questions: Why do you need it, when will you return, who is going to use it, and why HR is asking for a laptop for Accounts? To prove his loyalty, he may approach Mr. Naveen." *Now I understand why people say it's tough to work in India because people at each stage will try to stop you from going ahead.*

"By the way, why do you need an extra laptop?"

I narrated the entire incident of the morning.

"Oh, I see. You desperately need it. Ok, I'll get it done. I'll take it on your name with some sort of excuse. I can handle Krishna. I'll get you a laptop in next 10 minutes" *beautiful girls are always known to handle tough tasks easily.*

I came back to my workstation. All my colleagues were running desperately to finish the work before the deadline. I got on my seat and took one file. After 15 minutes, the laptop came to my workstation. Now, I was waiting for Murali to finish his chores and join hands with us.

"How you got the laptop from that husky giant Krishna?" I munched my bite.

"Don't make fun of him. He is a nice guy; just gets out of line sometimes. I gave him a requisition in your name that you have to finish your work for accounts since it's the last day before the deadline. You'll be working on both systems simultaneously"

"You said only this, and he agreed to give the laptop. Strange!" I was still figuring out how it happened.

"Mr. Arjun's looks always matter. A girl can get any guy to do anything with her looks," she gave me a sharp look.

"I am sorry dear. Because of me, you have to…"

"Stop it *yaar*. You needed the laptop for some wise reason, so I helped it. It wasn't for you, but for my company, so no thanks required"

"Shweta, I need one opinion from you." I have wanted to ask Shweta this for a long time.

"Dude, why do you behave like a stranger all the time? Outside the office, we are friends, at least I think so"

"Of course, we are friends—there is no doubt about it. But I was hesitating to ask you this, so I took your permission," I said.

"If you're thinking of proposing to me, then you have to go one-on-one with Vicky because he proposed to me last day." She laughed hard.

"What the F? That asshole never told me that he had gone a step ahead this time. Congrats, dear, so what have you decided?"

"There are some issues which we need to clear to each other before we take the road of Happy Journey"

"Oh, okay, but anyway, I was not proposing to you. I was indeed asking your opinion. About distance love," I popped it.

"Oh my God. Our dear Arjun is in love with a girl who is living in distance. What's her name dude? And how long have you been staying in such kind of feeling?" she winked at me.

"Her name is Sunaina. She is from Mumbai. A student of Fashion Design. We never saw each other. She will be coming to Bangalore soon to work on her project. We have been in talking terms since January this year. When I speak to her, I forget all my worries. She was the one who motivated me hard to take up the job. She has got a very sweet voice. A few months back, I realized I had developed some feelings for her. Like when I don't speak to her, I feel emptiness. Whenever I speak to her, I forget all my worries. I feel as if I am talking to my girlfriend, narrating the entire details of my day. She also does the same. I just wanted to know, whether it's love or infatuation" I was waiting for Shweta's diplomatic reply.

"Look, Arjun. Love is a feeling that can be seen or felt by you and not by any third person. Take your time. Don't jump to any conclusion. You guys have never seen each other, just chat over the phone. It's really hard to make views about any person whom you have never met in real. I do not doubt her. But I want you to be sure at first; do you really like her irrespective of her looks, colour, and faith? What if you find her not a good-looking?" Shweta had a point.

"How come looks came into the picture of Love?" I wanted to understand this.

"Ok, let me ask you something from a boy's perspective. Have you ever seen a guy fall in so-called love at first sight with an ugly-looking girl? I mean, a girl whose looks are not appealing," Shweta darted.

"To the extent I know, I never met a guy who fell in love at first sight with a less good-looking girl"

"Exactly. This is what I am trying to say. You're imagining that Sunaina is a damsel who would love you a lot and take care of you. What if you find that your imagination turns out unreal? She may not be a good-looking. Will you accept her?" Shweta was sounding aggressive.

"I never imagined Sunaina as a beautiful damsel, but I definitely got your point. Thanks for helping, dear. You're always the best help a friend can get," I said.

"Look, Arjun, I am sorry if you're hurt. But I know a guy's mentality. And I also know you're not one of that bunch. But still, I didn't want to witness a heartbreak neither for my bestie nor for the innocent girl."

"Don't be sorry dear. Whatever you said is completely practical. I would definitely think from this angle too. And if I am sure about this, I would propose to her," I finished my lunch.

"Now, let's get back to reality. You have a deadline to meet," Shweta reminded me of what I almost forgot. We left for the Office.

That was the most hectic day and night I witnessed. All of us were so engrossed in work that we almost forgot our office time for the day was over. Sheer dedication made me realize how much they respect and treat me as their own. Sharath was leaving his cabin. His face turned yellow when he saw all of us working hard to get things done. Maybe this is what people call leadership, he realized.

"Hi, Arjun; how is it going?" It was the first time he visited my desk.

"Going good, sir. I hope the deadline shall be met in the next hour," I proudly informed him.

"You can call me Sharath." Everyone, including me, was taken by surprise.

"Do you mind coming along with me in my cabin? I have something to say about it." Sharath led the way.

I followed him and closed the cabin.

"Firstly, I apologize to you for my arrogant behaviour. I know I did wrong to you. I was always harsh on you. You may say, I was jealous of you. That would be more accurate. I felt you were here to take away my position. I was scared. I don't know if you can understand it. Mr. Naveen is a North Indian, and you are too. I felt insecure about my position. People have a tendency to like people of their own caste, creed, or religion. Out of this insecurity, I never behaved well with you. I request you to accept my apologies."

*I couldn't believe what the lil monster was saying.*

"Sir, I can definitely understand your worry. Every person in our country fears this. If you're working under a North-Indian boss, you're worried because you may be ill-treated since you don't belong to his native or region. If I work under any South-Indian boss, the same fear would attract me. The basic reason is that we are divided by our regions rather than by our nationality. You may find Sikhs, Hindus, Muslims, Christians, Jains, Marathi, Gujarati, and Bihari, but hardly will you find a person who would introduce himself as Indian.

The political boundaries have made people distinguish between themselves" *I don't know how, but I felt I could be a philosopher too.*

"Thanks for understanding me, buddy. I promise to give you my full support in every work we do. Tomorrow, we will chalk out a plan to complete this financial responsibility." Sharath stood up to shake hands.

"I would support you in each and every work we do." I made a handshake and left the cabin.

Soon after this, Sharath left the office. My colleagues surrounded me as if I were trying to cross the border secretly and had been caught red-handed.

"What was he saying? Did he feel jealous of us that we have completed the task without his intervention?" Atul asked.

*I could sense he was mad at Sharath.*

"Nothing guys. He was saying that from the morning, we will sit for financial reporting work. Before that, I would like to thank each one of you for being so supportive and dedicated. I always knew that it's not so easy to do the work of ..." *Someone stopped my speech in the middle. It was Mani.*

"Wait a minute, Arjun. Please don't be in illusion. We did it because we wanted to teach Sharath a lesson that even at this age, we are dedicated. We have done nothing for you" The blunt-faced uncle hit me hard with his nonsense. *Bloody Uncle*

"Hi dude, how are you?" A late-night call instantly made me realize who it could be. It was Shruti.

"I am good, how are you?" I replied in sleep mode.

"I am also doing fine. Wake up, dude. I need something to talk about" Even though I was half-asleep, I could sense something was troubling her.

"What happened? Are you okay?"

"I am okay, but I have to ask you something. Sorry for ringing you so late"

"No worries, buddy. Tell me, what do you want to know?"

"Are you serious about Sunaina?"

"What? What made you talk about her at this odd hour?"

"I shall tell you about it, dude. Just tell me what you feel for her"

"To be frank, I am still trying to figure it out. Could you help me on this?"

"Yeah, Dumbo, you're always confused. Now tell me, what's your confusion?"

"In the noon, I was speaking to one of my colleagues, Shweta, about her. She told me to be assured whether I was in love or just an infatuation. She also said that most of the time, people fall in love because the girl has a pretty look, nice figure, blah-blah-blah"

"To me, I feel, to an extent, she is correct. Most of the time, people say I love you without even knowing what kind of person he/she is. Mostly, they say it is on the basis of looks. How come it has got any relevance with you?"

"Till date, neither I nor Sunaina have seen each other. I don't know what would happen if I find that she was not that good looking which I was imagining. Till yesterday, I was not surrounded by such feeling, but today after discussing it with Shweta, this topic is spinning over my head"

"To be frank, I would never like to indulge in such kind of serious matters, but since we are childhood buddies, I would try to help you. Just ask yourself at first, what do you want – A beautiful girl or a sensible girl?" Shruti said

"It would be great if the girl had a combination of both"

"Lol, for that, you need to try to arrange a marriage in some village 😜"

"To be frank, I would like to go with a sensible girl. Beauty might fade away, but not sensibility"

"Exactly, so come out of this illusion that she is very beautiful. Imagine she is a normal-looking girl, having no preferences towards beauty"

"Okay, I got your point"

"That's good, Mr. Arjun. Keep talking to her and try to find what she feels for you. Does she like you for the kind of person you are or for some other reason? Likewise, you also try to stay on the ground and don't think too much. If your heart says you should go with her, and then go with it"

"Thanks a ton, Shrutz, but why do you call me at such an odd hour?"

"Mom called me an hour back. She was looking damn serious about our relationship. I am already in love with a guy. His name is Akash. We met in college. He was my senior. Last year, he came to London to pursue his MBA, and so did I this year"

"Wow, you're such a badass. You didn't even tell me that you're roaming with a guy"

"I was a bit afraid, dear. When it was the farewell for our seniors, my boyfriend and I make out in the classroom"

"Make out what?" I knew what she meant, but I was trying to pull her legs.

"Nothing, Dumbo. I thought after having a gf, you might have grown up, but you're still the same. It was his wish that before he went to London, he would like to have sex with me. I was stressed those days. But he calmed me and promised me nothing will go wrong. We sneaked out during the farewell party, and I fulfilled his wish"

"you're really turning into a bad girl now. So how many times you have pleased him till date?"

"Excuse me, dude. I love him. And sex is just a part of Love. In London, it's very common. We almost have it twice a week" *I couldn't believe what she was saying.*

"Dear, you may be living in London, but your roots are connected to India. Think twice before you take any steps further. I am not feeling good about it, dear. I am sorry if you find my words ungenerous"

"Good night, dude, I will see you soon. Take care," and she kept the phone.

*I felt bad about it. I don't know, but I could smell something was not going right.*

"So, what you have decided for the future?" Dad asked me on breakfast.

"I have left it all on time. Let it decide my fate" I was blunt.

"A person without aim has no meaning in life. Why are you wasting your life's precious days on such kiddish things? Why don't you join my business?" I could sense his frustration.

"Dad, why are you so keen to take me to your business? You have said once that I am a useless guy and can't serve any purpose in your business. Didn't you?"

There was silence for a long time. My dad quietly left the table, and from the distance, I could see the droplets in my mom's eye. *Sometimes, I really feel these Saas-bahu serials should be banned. More than the actress, our ladies cry, and that too without glycerine.*

"Arjun, don't take me wrong. But your father is right. You need to set an aim in your life. What do you want to do ahead? Will you continue with your job or join the business? You need to decide quickly. Your father has worked really hard to get the family to such a comfortable level. I am not giving you any kind of lecture, but I am asking you to think upon this at least once." Uncle was sounding perfect.

"I know, uncle, but right now, I am so busy that I don't have any time to think about anything else except my work," I tried to escape.

"Arjun, it's your life. If you have no time to think about it, then I am really sorry to say you're marching towards a dead-end road where you'll find no option but to turn back and join the path again that you left earlier. I hope you're smart enough to get what I am saying" *I was caught. I felt so burdensome. A guy of age 23 has so many things to deal with. Love, Job, Business, Family, Friends. I almost forgotten this – Aim in life.*

"Arjun, what's compelling you not to join the family business?" uncle asked straight-forwardly.

"Nothing, Uncle. I feel I may not be the right person to handle the business with responsibility. I fear I might make some mistakes which may cause huge damage to the company. Also, I feel that I have nothing to do in the company since you and dad are taking care of it very well. The business is running at its best. What addition would I make?"

"I am surprised that you're thinking so low. Well, as far as your addition is concerned, you may add many things. You're a CA. You know more about taxation. Every day changes are happening in taxonomy, but we are not able to cope with it. It takes a long time for us to understand the provision of any law, and by the time we do it, we lose a hefty amount behind consultants and departments. You're young, energetic, and enthusiastic. You may bring new ideas to take this business to another level. From a traditional approach, you can turn it into modern thinking. It's not possible for me or for your dad to try out something new at this age. That's why we need a person from our family who can take the business to a whole new level." *It was the first time I ever realized how I could be an important asset to the company.*

"I agree with you, uncle, but please give me some time so that I can think about this perspective also." I tried to sneak away with an excuse since I was getting late.

"Sure, Arjun, but please consider this a priority. We would be very happy if you joined us on the board." Uncle took his last bite and left the table.

*It was the first time I saw my uncle taking Dad's side so keenly. Maybe I am my dad's only son, and hence, he would like to see me on board. Or maybe something is wrong, and my dad wants me to join it. I decided to give some time to it, but later. I was getting late for the office.*

"Hi, Sharath. Good morning." After reaching the office, I headed directly to Sharath's cabin.

"Good morning, Arjun. So, what's the status of pending entries?"

"All done. We have locked the back-dated entry beyond October 01"

"Good job Arjun. Now, let's move to the next level. Get the data for half a year in an Excel sheet. Once you're done with it, we will group the ledgers under respective heads. This would take a day or two times. Then, we would have to make some necessary adjustments, for which we would need the guidance of Mr. Naveen"

"Ok, Sharath, I will take the Trial balance extract and start working on it"

"Do you have knowledge of Advanced Excel, since you would be needing it very much to play with figures?" *I wanted to tell him – Dude, don't tell a Marwari how to play with numbers. He knew it before he entered this world.*

"Yeah, Sharath. In case I need any help, I would come to you"

"Anytime, Arjun. It is good to see that this time, we could beat the deadline. All thanks to you"

I left the cabin and came to my workstation. I was feeling energetic, as I was going to do something for the first time, which I always wanted to do. I extracted the Trial Balance for the half year from the system. All this we used to do in our accounts paper during exams, but this was real. A mistake of mine can change the basis of the decision of management. I was thrilled and excited to do it. Also, by the side, I was praying to God that nothing should go wrong.

◆

# Chapter – 13

"So, how is it going with you? Heard a good chemistry is cooking between you and Sharath" Shweta pinched me. We were out for lunch, as usual.

"Nothing like that dear. Last day he called me up in his cabin and asked me about the progress. I don't understand why you guys are so envious of him?"

"Dude, we've known him for a long time. You know, before you, there was another guy. He had to leave the job in just 8 months because of him. Beware of him; he is very cunning. He would try to make friends with you, and then he would strike as and when he gets the chance. Arjun, you're my friend. I don't want to see you in any trouble"

"Don't worry, Shweta. Let's talk something else. How is it going between you and Vicky?"

"It's going fine. He is a nice guy" *God, what has happened to the taste of girls? Vicky is a nice guy, in which aspect! Is she under some alcoholic influence?*

"You were saying that you need to clear out something with Vicky before you could move forward. What's the matter you wanted to speak to him?"

"Unless I speak about it to Vicky, I won't share it with you. I am really sorry, buddy, but please wait a while. I will tell you once I speak about it to Vicky"

"So what you're waiting for? Go and tell him what you need to share"

"Dude, I need some time"

"Okay"

"So, how is it going between you and Sunaina?"

"Going good. We have normal chat. These days we both are busy with our work. So, doesn't get much time to speak to her"

"Did you think about what I said last day?"

"Yeah. I felt you were right. I need to focus on my priority. Beauty or brain?"

"That's good dear. Don't take any decision in haste"

"Do you think pre-marital sex is fair enough in today's world?"

"Huh...How come this came across your mind? Are you fantasizing about something naughty?" she winked.

"No, dear. I am just asking. I have got no wrong intentions about Sunaina"

"Well, it depends. People do it for various reasons. Some are for the sake of love, and some think it's a need. For some, it's a kind of experiment, and for some, it's adventurous. And as far as my views are concerned, virginity has no connection with Love. If a person loves you, he will think beyond"

"But in our society, people still think that if a girl is not a virgin before marriage, she is not a good girl"

"Come on, Arjun, which era are you living in? Ok, tell me one thing. If a girl sleeps with someone else before marriage, it's wrong. What happened to that guy then?"

I was numb.

"Arjun, I understand our society is male-dominated. And hence, males would guard their interests. But please think from the point of view of a general person. If a girl is raped, she is blamed, even though it's not her mistake. But the guy, he comes out clean. It's easy to find that a girl is not a virgin, but is it possible with a guy?"

Silence. I was numb. Inside somewhere, I felt she was making her point, raising her voice for women's dignity.

"Arjun, pre-marital sex happens for many reasons. What we need is to know whether our partner is trustworthy or not. If a girl had an affair and had pre-marital sex, you might come to know about it. What if she has an affair at your back after the marriage? Will you ever come to know about it? I guess not a chance until you get a clue"

"Hmmmm, you're right. Sorry if you felt bad about something"

"No, dear, I didn't feel bad. If you have accepted that your POV needs a change, I have no issues"

"Fine, then let's move to office. Mr. Naveen would be waiting for us"

"Sure, we'll go. But why did you ask such a weird thing now?"

"Let's move, dear. When the right time comes, I will tell you." We proceeded to our office.

"Hi Sharath, I have extracted the trial balance in excel. But I need your help grouping them under the correct heads"

"Arjun, I am busy right now. Could you come after an hour?" A blank reply from the geek.

"OK, Sharath. I'll come after an hour." I marched towards my workstation. Shweta was talking to Atul when she saw me coming out of that geek's chamber with a dull face.

"What had happened, Arjun?" Shweta asked.

"Nothing, the geek said he is busy. He asked me to come after an hour. We are approaching our deadline, and this geek has no worries about it"

"Why he should be worried?" I was stunned to hear what she was saying.

"What are you saying? Mr. Naveen would take a jibe on us if we fail to meet the deadline"

"We? You're mistaking it, dude. I guess you have forgotten what Mr. Naveen said to you in his cabin. He asked you to do this task, not Sharath. Dude, we have warned you earlier also. He is playing politics with you. In the shield of financials, he would bring down your dignity in office. The good thing is all the entries you guys have done. Now, it's time for the finalization of accounts. You have got a week to do it"

*Shweta was damn right. It was my work; how did the geek enter this zone? Maybe I was asking too much favour.*

"Thanks a ton, dear. You literally saved me. I almost forgot whose task it was. I will make some arrangements to get out of this messy thing." I moved towards my workstation.

*For a moment, I realised that the condition of politics is much worse at the organizational level rather than the national level. You can't trust even your colleagues.*

I was trying to figure out how to proceed. I needed to finalize the financials in a week. All the entries were done, apart from adjustments. Now, I needed to put the ledgers into proper major heads and sub-heads as per Revised Schedule VI. Then, a solution clicked in my mind.

I obtained the previous year's financials with an Excel-linked trial Balance. I used some advanced Excel tricks and almost completed the classification except for a few. In an hour, I was done with the classification work, and I felt relieved. Now, the only major task was to convert these things into Revised Schedule VI format.

"Hi, Arjun; how is your work going?" Atul drops by my work-station.

"Almost done. Classification is done, now would prepare the notes to accounts and then link the same"

"Great, buddy. So, what help did geek provide you?"

*I was shocked to hear this. Even he calls Sharath a geek. Maybe it's the nick-name already given to Sharath before I could give.*

"Till now, only guidance," I informed Atul.

"Lucky you are. At least he guided you. Whenever we have asked for help, he bluntly refuses the same"

*I was almost blown away by what he said. I could understand that the geek won't help me because I belong to a different ethnicity, but why with others? They are all natives of the same state. Maybe Shweta quoted right for Sharath—cunning and smart-ass.*

"I don't understand one thing, Atul. You guys have been working here for a long time, but still, you guys don't have a good relationship with each other. Why is it so?"

"Arjun, it's not that we don't want to mingle with him. But most of the time, he plays foul with us. And because of this, we avoid him. He always tries to show the management that he is the only person who is working hard for the organization. Just because of greed and selfishness, he is ignored. Mr. Naveen also knows about this, but he doesn't have any other alternative. Sharath has a very good knowledge of taxation department matters. The only problem is he doesn't wish to share it with anyone"

"I see. Let's hope he doesn't play around with me. Anyways, major work is already done. Now, only the linking part is left. Hope we can finish the financials work in a few days"

"Definitely, you could do it. But still, as a colleague, I would warn you – Stay alert with Sharath. He may play games with you" Atul left the work-station. I also shut my system and packed my bag to leave for the day. Meanwhile, I was engrossed with thoughts regarding the scene going on in the office:

*What kind of place is this? People are entrusted to work hard and achieve the milestones set by the company. Instead, they start politicizing and polluting the environment. What kind of society are we living in? Is politics necessary for survival? Has it become a survival strategy for surviving at a job? Why do people need to go so down? Just to stay in the job and take all the grudges and jealousy on your colleagues. People always claim that they would never associate themselves with any form of politics, and now the same people are playing it well for survival. We always claim that politicians think of themselves first and then of the nation. How can we forget that we think of our position first and then we think about the aims and vision of the company? Will it be wrong to say that we have become insensitive and unsecured so much that we almost forgot our moral duty?*

I don't know when I reached the company parking lot. I saw my colleagues were leaving for the day happily and merrily. I could see the happiness bestowed on them once they realized they were heading back home. Why are they not so happy when they enter the office? Probably, either they have no work at home, or they have no political play at home.

"Hey dude, what's up? How was your day?" Sunaina was on the other side.

"I am good dear. What about you? How are you?"

"I am good. Hope your financial work is over by now"

"Not fully. You may say 70-80% is done. Rest shall be done in the next 1-2 days. I am quite sure that I'll meet the deadline"

"Oh, that's great. So, how is your love life going?"

"Pretty cool. My Love is offline right now. So, would you like to have a flirting session with me?"

"Oh my, Mr. Arjun knows how to flirt too?" I could hear her hard giggle.

"Don't worry, honey. I am pretty good at other things too"

"Like?" *There was a pause and, again, a hard giggle. I was enjoying every bit of it.*

"Well, all the things can't be explained over the phone. They are simply expressed when the person whom you love is in front of you"

"So, what are you planning to do, dear?"

"I have my plans. Just waiting for you to come to Bangalore"

"Dude, you are scaring me. I am really a nice girl"

"Ahm Ahm. So what? It doesn't matter to me if you're bad or nice. The only thing that matters to me is how you're going to feel it?"

"Oh, So Mr. Arjun knows how to scare people too? Good to see that. To be frank, I am really eager to come to Bangalore"

"Even I am eager to meet you"

"Why you're eager to meet me?" *A question that every girl would pop up to play mischievous as if they don't know the answer. Damn!*

"For the same reason, which is making you eager to meet me." *A diplomatic act always saves you, of course, but not for a longer time.*

"How do you know that my eagerness would be the same as yours?" *Damn, I told you guys, Diplomacy can save you only for a while. Girls of the modern era are really smarter.*

"Just guess it. By the way, do you have any wish list for your Bangalore visit?"

"Not yet. I have a duffer friend. So, he would be my guide"

"Alright. I shall chalk out the plan for you. Hope you like all these places"

"Dude, I am coming for project work, not for touring. So, please limit your plans within the city. Can I ask you something?"

"Dear, you don't need to be so formal. You may ask whatever you want to"

"Can I trust you?"

*A pause step into our conversation. I couldn't understand how this came into the middle. What made her ask such a question? Does she doubt me? Or maybe we haven't met ever, so she is a bit reserved on this? Before I could say, she broke the pause.*

"Look, I am sorry for asking you this, but I hope you can understand. We have never met. We have been talking over the net and phone for the past 7-8 months. We never know whom we are speaking to on the other side. Is he a Gentleman or a Demon? I know you are feeling bad about it, but I had to ask this. Can I trust you?"

"Yes, you can trust me. Look, I totally understand your concern. And probably, the cases happening around the globe against a woman would definitely generate a cause of concern. Don't feel bad at all, dear. I am happy that you asked this. Even if you have any doubt, you may call off the meeting"

"Don't be so rude. I am not going to call this meeting off. I really want to meet you, and I hope you, too, find it safe to meet me." A laugh busted.

"Hey dude, I got to go. See you later. Bye dear, take care"

"You too, buddy, take care, see you later"

*I could feel how happy I was. She would be coming to Bangalore in just a few months. How am I going to speak to her? Will she like me? What if she doesn't like me? Should I express my feelings in our first meeting? Do boys always get confused like this when it's about love?*

◆

# Chapter – 14

"Hi, Arjun. Could you please update me on the status? What is going on right now?" The geek asked me.

"Sharath, I have completed the task of grouping. Now, I just need to link it with the notes, and then the financials will be ready on my end. I just need a couple of guidance from you. What are the adjustments we need to make?"

"Arjun, you are going at a very high pace. What are your intentions? Are you going to take my place?" *The geek said with a soft smile. It was hard to understand his expression—was he jealous, or was he trying to pull my leg?*

"No, Sharath, nothing like that. How could I take this seat of yours? I am just a kid in front of you" *Thanks to diplomacy, I was able to handle this guy.*

"Hmmm, we would sit in the afternoon to check the things out. Till then, you finish the task of linking and do some ledger scrutiny"

"Ledger Scrutiny? What's this?"

"What, you don't know what is ledger scrutiny?" He gazed at me in such a manner that I felt it was a must-thing for any CA.

"Nope, I never came across such a thing ever"

"I doubt whether you have done your article ship properly. It's really hard to believe that a CA like you doesn't know about Ledger Scrutiny"

This time the geek took on my nerves. I remembered well what Atul told me last day. Since I needed to complete my work, I just listened to whatever the crap he said.

"Sharath, could you please help me with this thing? I really have got no idea about it"

"Of course, if I don't help you, you may get a good reason in front of Mr. Naveen to say that you were not able to complete the task"

"What's wrong with you? Why you're thinking so low? Did I say that I'll complain to Mr. Naveen?" *The prick was rising on my nerve. It was really hard to control myself.*

"Fine, dude, I guess you don't need my help. Do your work well. I have some other tasks to do. See you later"

*I was surprised. The geek was behaving very rudely. If it wasn't the office, I would have kicked his butt so hard that he would have never dared to misbehave with anyone. Still, I had no choice.*

"Sharath, I am sorry if you're hurt for any reason. We need to finish this task, and only you can tell me how to finish this task" *I assumed he understood I was pleading.*

"Look Arjun, if your senior says something, you must take it in a positive way. Don't be so arrogant. You may have cleared your CA in first attempt, but still you need to learn many things" *Sharath flaunted his seniority.*

"I got it Sharath. I'll do as you say" I didn't want to continue this argument unnecessarily.

"Fine, first of all, take all the ledgers of Assets side, study them properly, and find if there is any mistake. Check if any entry is missed out on any part, specially the provisional entries"

"But I have got no idea of provisional entries. Which Account shall we consider for passing the provisional entries?"

"Please Arjun, I guess we are doomed. I thought you're capable enough to handle this task, so I didn't interfere much in this matter. But now, I guess we have to apologise to the management that we are unable to meet our deadline. If you didn't know how to do the task, why did you take it?"

*This time he rang the bell.*

"Listen Sharath, you might be aware of the fact that nobody likes you in this office. Because of your arrogance and attitude, you have earned a bad repo in the office. And to be very honest, I have done my part very well. Provisional entries and adjustments shall be made by you, and this has been discussed earlier. As far it is concerned about the management, I can provide a well explanation about the failure to meet deadline. What explanation would you provide? I know you like playing politics and you have eliminated several good people from the office, just to secure a position for your fat ass. But remember dude, if you try mess with me, I'll forget my etiquettes, and you'll have my wrath" *I didn't realize how I got so much of courage to speak all this. But after hearing me down, the face of geek turned pale.*

"Arjun..."

"Just shut up. That day when you were talking to me as a friend, I felt you really mean it. But now I get to realize that everybody is right about you. You're a big-time loser. Just to keep yourself in the company, you have destroyed career of many young professionals. Don't you feel shame on yourself when you see the mirror every day?"

"Arjun lets sort it out. We must talk on it rather than fighting. We both are professionals"

"Dare not you call yourself professional? If playing politics in office is a profession, then I would request you to join the politics. Hope you would respect your profession very well"

I left the cabin, and I saw my colleagues were standing right outside the cabin.

"What's the matter? Have you guys got no work?"

"We do have Arjun, but we have never witnessed someone taking on Sharath so hard. You jacked him very well" Mani came forward and shook my hands.

"Really Arjun, you have done the task which none of us have ever expected" Padmini also came forward and shook my hands.

"Guys relax. It wasn't a war kind of thing. Don't take your colleagues as your enemy. He is also a human. If he does something wrong, we must try to correct him, rather than trying to take revenge on him. We must co-operate with each other and work in the direction to achieve company's goal rather"

All of them staring at me as if I have gone mad, or I have turned into a spiritual leader and giving them the advice at free of cost.

"Well said Arjun. After a long time, I feel we have got a right candidate who is away from any sort of politics" It was Atul.

"Let's get back to work, and Atul, I need a help from you. Could you please come to my work-station?"

"Yes Arjun"

"Heard you have created a mess in office today?" Shweta cheekily asked me.

"Oh, so you also got to know what had happened"

"Of course, Arjun. I also got to know about your motivational speech, why don't you try becoming a spiritual leader?"

"Stop it *yaar*, nothing like that. I don't understand why the geek was behaving so different? The other day he promised me to work with co-operation, and today it was totally a different picture"

"You still didn't get it Arjun. How many times you want us to explain you that Sharath is an unpredictable guy. If he has some work with you, he will stand with you; else you are nobody for him. Leave him for a while. You tell how your internet friend is?"

"She is fine, concentrating towards her upcoming project in Bangalore. We have planned to meet. Let's see what happens"

"Hey that's great dear. So, are you clear with your confusion?"

"Dear, I have stopped thinking about this. It's true I like chatting with her, and I find her company very pleasing. But I would like to depend on my conscience this time. If my heart would say go ahead, I will tell her"

"Cool. But you're not sounding romantic"

"I know, dear; I am not that romantic. But yes, I can take good care of my love"

"Oh ho, Mr. Arjun seems to be in love then."

"Hmmm...You may say so, dear. By the way, how is it going on between you and Vicky"

"Things are fine. He is a nice guy and understands me well. We will be meeting this Sunday in Sky High Pub. He said he has got some surprise for me."

"Oh, that's great. But you said you have something to tell him before you go ahead with this relationship. Have you said it?"

"Nope, I have a plan to say it soon. When I feel I should tell him everything about myself, I won't wait for any special moment"

"Hmm...That's great. Let's move back to the office. Our Lunch time is already over." We got up and walked towards the office.

"By the way, how are you going to complete your task? Tomorrow is the last day. You need to submit your data a day after tomorrow"

"Just wait and watch, dear. I have made my arrangements," and we walked towards our office.

"Arjun, what is the status of Financials? Are they ready at your end?"

On the 16th day, Mr. Naveen called Sharath and me to his cabin. Sharath's face was full of tension.

"Yes, Sir, it is already. We just needed to discuss some provisional entries. Once we are clear with this, the financials are ready"

"Good. Bring the print-outs of the financials and forward me the Excel-linked trial balance. Sharath, have you done the Ledger scrutiny?"

"Sir, actually..."

"Yes, Sir, it is done"

"Arjun, Sharath can speak, so let him speak. Tell me, Sharath, have you done the ledger scrutiny?"

"Yes, Sir. I have already done it," Sharath said.

"Good, get me the details." He signalled us to get the documents he had asked for.

"Arjun, I haven't done the ledger scrutiny, so why do you say Ledger scrutiny done?"

"Because I have already done it for you" His expression could be easily read. He was shocked to hear this.

"Who did it? You didn't know about it?"

"You're right, I didn't know about it. But I had the willpower to take up this challenge and do it. I'll inform you everything, but let's finish our meeting with Mr.

Naveen first" We walked towards my workstation and took the details out as required.

"I can't believe it; you did it on your own. Do you have any findings with regards to Ledger scrutiny?" Sharath was still perplexed.

"Yup, Sharath, I have the findings. I can tell you that many of the findings belong to the previous year. We have corrected them and taken the ledger printouts for the current year's entries. You're safe"

*I could say the geek was about to cry. His eyes became moist. Maybe he was feeling ashamed of what he had done in the past with me and other colleagues. His expression went dull. He was speechless.*

"You have the opportunity to get me jacked in front of Mr. Naveen. Still, you didn't do it. Why were you so gentle when I was so harsh to you?"

"Because I am just your colleague, not a politician. And it wasn't only me who helped you out. It's the whole Accounts department. It was you who taught Atul once about Ledger scrutiny, and he helped all of us to get it done. We worked for two days continuously to achieve our targets. Working in harmony gives you more pleasure and power rather than working with politics. Sharath, we all know how scared you are for your position, but it doesn't mean you play games against them and chuck them out of the office" *As soon as I finished, the geek was in tears. He came forward and hugged me and cried for a while. The whole Accounts department was in awe. They couldn't believe what they were seeing.*

"It's ok Sharath. Right now, we have to finish this task. Mr. Naveen would be waiting for us"

Hearing this, Sharath calmed down, and we walked towards Mr. Naveen's cabin.

"Sir, I have mailed you the Excel file, and here are the documents"

I submitted the file containing the print-outs and other necessary working documents to him to vouch for the details of the financials. After an hour of discussion and vouching, Mr. Naveen accepted the financials and asked us to leave.

"Arjun, I can never forget this kindness of yours. I owe you, and I promise whenever you or any of the colleagues would need my help, I will be there for you guys"

*I was relieved. Finally, we had changed the geek's thought process. As we walked towards our department, he apologized to each member and assured them of his all-time support.*

"I am sorry to all of you. I was always selfish and tried to put you guys down in front of management. But today, you guys have saved me from the mess. I was egoistic, and arrogant, but still, you people did well for me. I apologize to each and every one of you. And I assure you guys, whenever you need my help in any form, I will always stand by your side. Thanks again to all of you."

"There is no need to thank us, Sharath. It was Arjun who changed our minds, and he did yours, too. He cleared our consciences and explained to us that goals are more important than enmity. We must work in peace and harmony so that we can give our best to our organization," Mani replied.

"Sure, Mani *Anna*, we would work in peace and harmony and ensure that politics never divided us again." Sharath walked back to his cabin.

Everybody came forward and greeted me for the change.

"Thanks a ton, Arjun. We never expected this would happen. You made the dream come true. We will always be grateful to you," Atul smiled.

"Whatever I have done is my job. We are here to work, not to fight. Let's not get touched by the political environment and disturb the peace amongst us".

"Hope this remains forever in this office," Padmini greeted me.

"Definitely, it will." I smiled and walked towards my workstation, and so did others.

Time elapsed quickly, and the day was about to approach when I would be meeting my lady love the other day. She had already forwarded me her accommodation details along with her journey details. We planned to meet at CCCD in Indiranagar as it was falling convenient for her. Later in the evening, I got a knock on my door. It was the devil in disguise of Friend – Ankit

"Hey bro, wassap?" he greeted me at the door.

"Nothing much, buddy. It's good you drop down here."

"Why? What happened? Did you have a heartbreak once again? Shall we go to some bar again?" *I knew the asshole was trying to pull my legs.*

"No, buddy. Do you remember Sunaina? She invited me to meet her tomorrow at CCCD in Indiranagar"

"Damn sure, it must be your choice to meet there"

"It's not what you're thinking. The place would be convenient for her to reach. So I chose the destination. And moreover, CCCD is a very decent place"

"I know CCCD is a decent place, and you love that place like your soul," he giggled.

"Anyways, that's not the point. Look, Sunaina and I have been speaking to each other for the past year. And I feel I am in love with her. I know it would sound ridiculous to you that how can a person fall in love with another just by talking over the phone or net"

"No, I am not thinking that. I am thinking that you have already tasted the burns; still you want to play with fire. You are on the verge of proving the proverb wrong – A burnt child dreads the fire. Look, Arjun, I know you very well. If a girl goes nice with you, you develop a feeling for her. But are you sure it's truly the feeling of love?"

"You know, I have been battling with the same for the past 5-6 months. Do I love her, or is it just an infatuation? If it was an infatuation, it would have gone away by this time. I really enjoy her company. Whenever she smiles, a bell rings in my heart. Her voice makes me forget all my apathy. I know it's not easy to go ahead with these reasons, but I really adore her"

"Dude, even then, I would suggest – don't be in haste. Take your time, understand the girl. If you find that your feelings towards her are genuine, don't waste the moment."

"Thanks, buddy. I hope all goes well tomorrow"

"Sure, Dude. Things would be fine. Just try to be you. Hope you find your true love. Now, let's make a move.

Others are waiting at tea point." ◆

# Chapter – 15

Finally, the day came to meet Sunaina. The traffic horns honked behind me, bringing me back to my senses. I was anxious and nervous to meet her. I reached CCCD half an hour earlier. The place was, as usual, surrounded by young couples and a college-going crowd. Whenever I visit CCCD, my college day memory refreshes. It is the ultimate place to get nostalgic.

I was lost in my thoughts when my phone buzzed.

"Hello, Arjun, where are you?"

*It was Sunaina.*

"I am in CCCD. Where are you?"

"Would be reaching in another five minutes. See you there"

"But how would you recognize me?"

"Don't worry, I will find you out. See you," and the call was disconnected.

*This time, I was feeling too nervous. I had waited for this moment all the time, and now my hands were cold. I felt I was freezing. My heartbeat was running like a speedometer. The world seemed hazy to me.*

"Hi, if I am not wrong, are you Arjun?"

*A sweet voice brought me back to the real world. A girl, dressed fashionably, was standing in front of me. She was wearing one of those peplum kinds of black dresses. Her hair was smooth, straight, and black. Her lips were bright, and her eyes were shining. Her cheeks were round and seemed to be soft. She was looking like a fashionista. It wasn't hard for me to guess – it was my dream girl, my online-cum-offline friend – Sunaina.*

"Hi Sunaina" I greeted her gently and stood to pull the chair for her.

"Thanks Arjun. I thought you would take moments to recognize me, but you did it in a fraction of a second. Glad to see this"

"It's all my pleasure. Hopefully, you liked my city"

"I haven't seen it yet; I hope you can show me something special in Bangalore that makes me inclined towards it."

"Uhm, sure. But before that, let's order something"

"Arjun, let's wait for some time. We will order the food a little later"

*She was constantly looking at me. I was unable to hide my blushing. I guess she noticed it. We stayed mute for a while as neither of us knew how to proceed. We kept looking at each other. Finally, I broke the ice.*

"You're looking ravishing in this outfit. It suits you."

"Thank you, Mr. Arjun. I thought you were going to be silent throughout the day," she giggled.

"Nothing like that Sunaina. I was a little nervous. So I was silent"

"It's ok dude. It happens with guys when they meet a beautiful girl like me"

*This time we both giggled.*

"By the way, how did you recognize me? I didn't give you any hint"

"You fit completely into my version of imagination. The way I imagined, you were looking exactly the same. The smart, handsome, dashing dude"

*She laughed out hard. I was unable to make out what made her laugh so hard – her imagination came true or the look on my face.*

"How is your project going on?"

"Dude, I am here to meet you, not to tell you about my projects and other things. To be frank, the Project was just an excuse. I came here to meet you"

*I was happily shocked. What was that? The girl had travelled more than 500 km to meet me and look at me, sitting like an idiot.*

"I can't believe what you just said. You came here to…"

"Yes, to meet you. I travelled from Mumbai to Bangalore. I know you might be thinking this girl has gone crazy, and to an extent, I have gone"

"But we could have met later also. Destiny would have surely planned for it."

"Destiny is what you make, not what it makes you. I wanted to meet you, so I came. For me, this is the destiny. What do you think?"

"I think you're crazy," and we laughed out loud.

"So it was your sole purpose to visit Bangalore?"

"Let the perfect time come. I will tell you about it. Let's order something. I am feeling hungry now"

We called up the waiter and ordered some snacks and espresso coffee.

"So, you took a leave for the day?" she inquired.

"Of course, after all, you travelled such a long distance for me," I winked at her.

"Hahaha...nice joke dear. So how's your work going on?"

"Dear, I have come here to meet you, not to discuss my office life." It was my time to giggle.

"Nice, so Mr. Arjun knows how to settle the score?"

"All credit to you. So, how many days your project will continue?"

"As long I want"

"I didn't get you."

"You don't need to get it, dear. Just tell me, what you have got for me?"

*Suddenly, I remembered about the gift which I had bought for her. I pulled it out from my bag.*

"This is for you. Hope you like it"

"Hahahahaha...thanks for the gift dear. But actually, I meant, what are the things you have planned out?"

"Ohhh. No worries. I have my plans. So, when should I pick you up tonight?"

"I'll be free by 7.30. You can pick me up by 8. By the way, where will you be taking me?"

"As I said, it is a surprise for you"

"Hope it turns out to be good enough"

"It would"

*Meanwhile, the guy came up with our order. But I was busy noticing her. I could see in her eyes; she was very happy to meet me. Her face was lightening more than the brightness of the sun. She appeared to be so fresh. Her innocent face could melt the heart of a rock. My eyes were transfixed on her sharp nose. The nose ring added more beauty to the sharp nose.*

"Hey dude, you there?"

"Uh, Yeah. Why, what happened?"

"I have been calling your name. But God knows where your mind was wandering?"

"Nothing like that dear. I was lost in my thoughts. Let's have it"

*We took out cups and bites. I was unable to take my eyes away from her. She noticed it.*

"Hey dude, what's wrong with you? Are you ok? Any health issues?"

"Nope, I am alright. I am just mesmerized by your beauty. You're looking pretty"

"Thank you. Now, enough of it. Let's talk something else. So, how's everyone at your place?"

"All are good. Dad is busy with his business; Mom is busy in her womanish chit-chat. What about people at your side?"

"All are good. In fact, I am having less interaction with my dad and brother. They are too busy with their practice. Luckily, you're not practicing."

*We looked at each other and smiled. I don't know what it was—whether I was nervous or too shy to ask her anything—but I was ruining my impression.*

"Heard enough of Mumbai's nightlife. How's it?"

"It's damn good. People keep walking for 24 hours. The city never sleeps. Since I am a fashion student, I have attended several parties. So, it's not new for me. The best part is many of the top fashion designers are based in Mumbai, so I love attending the parties for interaction"

"Nice dear. So, am I your only online-cum-offline buddy?"

"Sorry I didn't get you"

"I mean, am I the only friend whom you met on the internet?"

"Till date, yes. The best part about you is whatever I expected, you're the same"

"I hope you expected something good only"

"Yeah. Tell me one thing, don't you miss Riya?"

*Out of nowhere, she landed the bomb.*

"Dear, it was a past. I have moved on. And I really don't want to think about the past"

"Hmmm. Dude, I need to leave now. I will meet you at 7:30. I'll message you my pickup address. And I hate waiting," she smiled.

"Don't worry, madam. Chauffer would be at your service on time"

*We giggled hard. I signalled for check. The guy brought the bill. I handed him my credit card.*

"It was lovely meeting you. Whatever the fear I had before the meeting, it has all vanished. Thanks for being so gentle"

"The pleasure is all mine. It was so nice of you that you travelled so far to meet me. Thanks a ton." The guy brought back my card, and we were ready to leave.

"Which way you shall be going? Shall I drop you?"

"No, it's perfectly fine. I'll take an auto. I'll see you in the evening. Let's see which place you have planned for me"

"Definitely, you'll like the place if you like to party."

"Arjun, if you don't mind, I would like to meet where we can talk easily. No sound, no disturbances"

"Cool, I have a place in my mind. You would fall in love with that place"

"Great, then see you in the evening"

"Hi dude, how was your meeting?"

"No idea. I was literally lost in her beauty. Her eyes were so deep that I couldn't come out of it"

*My teacher and love guru – Ankit, was on a call.*

"As usual, you failed my child. If I was the girl, I would have rejected you instantly. Why do you get so nervous? What did she say?"

"She said she enjoyed the time spent with me. We shall be meeting in the evening. She wants to meet at a quiet place"

"So which place have you decided? And what did she say about the gift?" The *idea and choice belonged to Ankit.*

"Dude, don't be nuts. Why shall she open it in front of me?"

"You never know. You may find people like me. Ok, leave it. Which place you have decided for her?"

"I am still figuring it out. I have a place in my mind. I just need to check it"

"Name the place dude?"

"Persian terrace at Hotel Sheraton"

"Awesome choice. If possible, book the poolside table. Ask them to arrange it according to a date"

"Yup, I'll check with them. I'll see you later"

"All the best dude. If you require the help of any sort, I am just a call away"

"I know, buddy." I disconnected the call. Sometimes, it makes you feel so proud that you have the best people on the globe around you.

"Hi, Arjun. Have you got my message for pickup?"

"Yup, I have got it. I shall be there in another half an hour. I'll give you a call once I reach the destination"

"Ok, dude. See you"

*Finally, I was able to convince my dad to let me drive his SUV tonight. Every moment, I checked myself in the side mirror. I was too cautious about my looks. I kept a perfume bottle beside my seat. I reached my destination on time.*

"Hi Sunaina, I have reached the place. Where are you?"

"I shall be coming in a minute or two"

"Ok, dear. No problem. I am in an SUV car numbered 6386"

"Cool, dear. See you"

*I took the bottle, applied it over my suit, and kept it in a drawer. I checked my hair, and they looked sexy and at peace. I checked the smell of my breath. It was cool. Not that I have any plan to kiss her, but one should be ready in a complete manner for a date. I watched her coming. She was looking much wow. The dress I gifted her was fitting her in an absolute sense. She looked like a princess in a white Western. I was unable to take my eyes again. She came to the car and knocked on the door. I realized it and opened the gates.*

"Arjun, I guess next time I shouldn't dress properly"

"Why is it so?"

"Every time you lose your concentration and forget about everything"

*We giggled.*

"I know you're bored to hear this, but you're looking like a princess"

"Thanks for the compliment. And no matter how many times you say about a girl's beauty, she would always love to hear it"

*We smiled and started to move towards the Persian terrace.*

"So, tell me something about the place we are going"

"Just wait for some time. The place is exactly the way you want. Simple and quiet, yet appealing. Just like you"

"Hello, dude; I may be a simple girl, but I am not at all quiet"

"Yeah, true." I smiled.

We kept chit-chatting for a while before we reached the destination. A person came to Sunaina's side and opened the door for her. He handed her something wrapped in a gift pack.

"Thank you, but what's this?"

"Madam, this shall be answered once you reach the table"

She looked at me with curiosity, but I pretended to be unaware of it. I handed my keys to the valet parking. We started moving towards the entrance. A guy, dressed neatly, came to Sunaina and handed her another gift wrap.

"What's this?"

"Madam, you shall learn about this once you reach your table."

She looked perplexed and asked me about this whole. I denied knowing anything about it.

"What's going on, Arjun? What are these gift wraps?"

"As the person said, you'll get to know about this once you reach the table. So let's move"

We took the elevator, and the person inside again handed her a gift wrap. She knew what the person would say if she asked what this was, so she decided to wait until she reached the table.

The elevator stopped on each floor, and a person on each floor handed her a gift wrap. Finally, we reached the table. The place was decorated as it was asked to. A table with white linen cloth was parked beside the swimming pool on the rooftop. Two candles were placed on the table, and the aroma made the atmosphere look romantic. A small basket was kept between the two candles, which had some fresh fruits and a bottle of champagne. Four people were standing to surround all the corners of the table with guitars. The manager came to receive us and guided us to reach the table.

Just as we started to move on, we realized petals were being showered on us from the top. The petals were of red and white roses. We were slowly holding each other's hands. I realized it was the best moment I had witnessed in my life. I could see the happiness on Sunaina's face. My God! She was blushing.

We reached the table. I pulled the chair for her. On the chair, a card was kept.

"What's this, Arjun?"

"Check it out. But I would suggest you to see it later. Let's enjoy this splendid evening"

She smiled and kept the card near the table. The manager attended to us.

"A beautiful Good evening to you, Ma'am. The whole arrangement has been made at the request of Mr. Arjun. After the dinner, there is a surprise planned for you, Ma'am. I would take your leave and send my person to care for your needs."

"Thanks a lot. The arrangements are lovely," Sunaina replied.

With a smile, the Manager left. Sunaina turned towards me. We looked into each other's eyes. Her hair was left open, and hence, they came near her face, adding red to her beauty. Her lips were glossy and sexy. Her eyes were still, but I could feel they were trying to say many things. After a while, she spoke.

"Arjun, I can't believe this. You did it all for me. What should I say? Maybe, Thanks for this lovely date"

"The pleasure is all mine. But something more special is there for you. I hope you will like it."

"Like it? I shall love it. I have never felt so special ever. Thanks for the beautiful evening."

A waiter came to our table and asked for permission to open the champagne. After the nod, he pulled up the cork and poured it into our glasses.

"I never thought you would be so romantic. I am not finding any words to say how good I am feeling right now"

"No words required. I can read your eyes. I am happy 'coz you're happy"

The people around our table were playing guitar and making the environment more melodious. I stood up from my table and went near to her on my feet.

"May I have an opportunity to dance with the most beautiful girl on this planet?"

She couldn't say anything except blushing. I took her hands in mine gently, and we walked towards the dance floor. She kept her hands on my shoulder, and I kept mine on hers. Slowly, I put my hands around her waist and brought her near to me. I could feel her sensuous breath. I could feel her heartbeat. She gently raised her eyes and gazed at my eyes. We kept looking at each other for moments. We have forgotten about everything. I felt as if we were alone on an undisclosed island. Slowly, we started moving our feet. The warmth of her hands was making me more romantic. My eyes were transfixed on the dimples on her cheeks. I wanted to kiss those pretty cheeks.

"Arjun, I must say you have a good taste. You chose a beautiful place and made it more romantic"

"Thanks, Sunaina. But something more interesting is waiting for you ahead"

We kept holding each other till the music stopped. We proceeded back to our table, and the waiters came forward to serve the dishes.

"Wow, the appetizers are so yummy. The sizzlers are just wow. I have no words to say. This is the best evening of my life"

I was glad to hear that. We finished the delicious dinner when the manager attended to us.

"I hope you enjoyed this beautiful evening Madam"

"Thanks for the lovely arrangements. It was really nice. The courteous staff of yours made it much better"

"Shall we proceed for another surprise?"

"Where is that?"

"Please come with me"

We got up to walk along with the manager. Sunaina slowly whispered

"I am really excited to view the next surprise. Could you give me any hints about it?"

"The only hint I can give you is that it will bring down the whole world under your feet"

She was perplexed. The manager took us to an open ground. We reached the venue.

"Oh my God, it's a hot air balloon." A wide smile appeared on her face.

"As I told you, the whole world would be under your feet tonight."

We smiled and slowly approached the balloon, holding her arms in mine. We got into the balloon and signalled to be taken off. The balloon was lit, and slowly, it began taking off.

"Oh my God, it's really the best surprise, Arjun. I never felt so special. I cannot explain how I am feeling right now," she said, opening her arms to hug me.

I slowly embraced her in my arms. We were silent for minutes, feeling each other's heartbeats and trying to feel them. I kept my hands around her waist, and she kept on mine. Slowly, I moved my hands near her shoulder to look at her face. Her eyes were closed. Her lips were silent. The soft air was trying to say something in her ears. Slowly, she opened her eyes and looked at me. We were able to read each other's minds. More than our lips, our eyes were talking. I gently put my hands around her waist again and brought her closer to me. I could feel her heartbeat running at pace. We got closer to each other. I gently held her in my arms. Slowly, we closed our eyes, and our lips met. I could feel the freshness. She let out a soft moan. Slowly, I brought my hands near to her breast and pressed them slowly. She put her palm around my hair and started curling it. Our smooch became passionate this time. It was hard for us to realize anything that was happening. Our hands weren't free. We were lost in each other. Our arms disagreed with parting away. Slowly, our lips parted. For me, it was the most memorable evening. I saw her face. She was blushing. We were not saying anything, just listening to our hearts.

After the completion of the round, the balloon safely landed at its place. We got out of it, and the manager came forward to receive us.

"I hope you have enjoyed our special surprise."

Sunaina looked at me and said, "Yes, I enjoyed it. I felt the whole world came below my feet."

"Thanks a lot for giving us a chance to serve you, Sir. I hope to see you soon again," he escorted us to our car. We took our seats. I started to drive to drop Sunaina at her place.

"I hope you liked it," I asked Sunaina.

"What - the evening or the smooch?" she winked at me.

"Both," we smiled.

"Both of them were amazing. You made me feel special today."

We stayed mute for the rest of the time. Maybe we were busy recounting the moments we had on our most memorable evening. We reached the hotel where Sunaina was staying. I got out of my seat and opened the door for her. She came out and gently closed the door.

"So, our evening ends," I said.

"Not yet. I, too, have got some surprise for you."

I was perplexed.

"The surprise is in my room. I would insist you come."

I gave my car for parking and started walking with her to her room. She took out the card and swiped it on the machine outside the room. The door was unlocked. We entered the room. It was neat and sophisticated. She gently locked the door.

"So, where is my surprise?" I asked with mischief.

"On its way. Have patience, Mr. Arjun," she replied innocently.

"Just give me a moment; I shall be back with surprise."

She went into the washroom. I sat on her bed. My mind was busy thinking about the surprise. I looked around but found nothing. With a sound of creak, the door opened. Sunaina came out in a lacy dress. The outfit made her look sexier. I was amazed to see her in this avatar. She walked towards me gently. She bent down a little and gently kissed my lips. They parted soon.

"I am giving you what I have got," she said, pulling a string away. The dress kissed Collin on the floor.

"Sunaina, I don't..."

"Arjun, I don't know what you have got in your mind. But I wanted to pour my heart out today. I LOVE YOU. I love you a lot. Words would fall short to describe my love for you. I wanted to tell you this long back, but I held myself so that I could be sure about you. I have been struggling with this for the past 03 months, to tell you, but I was scared a bit. I wanted to meet you and tell you. Thankfully, I got the chance to come to Bangalore because of the project. I would accept whatever decision you would take."

I got up and held her hands in mine.

"Sunaina, I can't tell you how much I love you. You lit my mood when I was feeling low at our first chat. You supported me all the time I needed you. You have been there with all my odds and evens. Like you, I was also in two minds, but now I am pretty sure. I love you. Would you like to be with me and support me in all the ups and downs of my life?"

"Yes. I would." We hugged each other. Her eyes were moist. The room went silent. My hands were running over her naked body. I could feel the heat. She was breathing heavily, and so was I. Our eyes met. I could see the ocean of love in her eyes. She surrendered to me in entirety. I took her in my arms and took her on the bed. I began kissing her forehead, cheeks, and nose. I came on top of her, and she held me tight. Soon, we locked our lips. It was a never-ending one. Our tongues started playing and aroused us more. My hands were locked with her hands. Slowly, I moved down and grabbed one of her nipples under my lips. She let out a moan. She held my hair tight. I went down to her navel and kissed it softly. She pulled me back and locked our lips. She began unbuttoning my shirt. My trouser was tossed on the edge of the bed.

"Are you sure you want to do this?" I asked.

"I don't know about it, but if I want to do this with anyone, it would be you," she responded.

We hugged each other tightly. She let me in with ease. We made love. Our souls are united at this very moment. We fell asleep in each other's arms.

We woke up after some time. I looked at her. She seemed happy, so I kissed her again.

"Do you have any repent for what we just did?" I asked.

"Nope, not a one."

We got up and dressed ourselves. I bid her bye with a gentle kiss on her lips. I reached my car and drove home. All the way, I was thinking about the moment we had. I loved her surprise.

# Chapter – 16

"So, how was your date?" Shweta asked me once we grabbed our chairs for lunch.

"It was good. She liked my gifts and surprises."

"Cool. So, what all you did for her?"

I told her about the evening we spent at the Persian Terrace.

"Wow, amazing dude. I wish Vicky also does the same for me."

"Definitely, he would do. So, how is it going between you guys?"

"Going great"

"You said you have got to clear out something. Is it cleared?"

"Not yet. Waiting for the right time."

"I want to ask you a personal question. May I?"

"Please go ahead."

"Do you love Vicky?"

"Yes. I do"

*I never expected it would come so soon. I knew Vicky was not a badass, but I had never seen him get serious with any girl. I was really worried—what's going to happen next?*

"Good. I guess you guys must talk first before proceeding ahead. Wish u luck."

"Thanks, dear. Did you tell Sunaina about your feelings?"

"Yup, she also has the same feeling for me."

"Wow, dude, you're so lucky. When are you going to introduce us to Sunaina?"

"Very soon"

"Great. Hope you get lucky this time."

"I, too, hope for this."

"So, how's it working with Sharath & Co.?"

"It's smooth now. Rather than senior-junior, we treat each other as friends."

"Great. I could see the change in wind."

"Yeah, things are getting into favour at this moment."

"Nice. Dude, tell me one thing. Your family was looking for a match with one of your family friend's daughter. Will your family accept Sunaina instead of her?"

*I know how she knew about Shruti. Damn, Vicky!*

"I and Shruti are just good friends. We have no such feelings for each other. Moreover, she has a boyfriend whom she loves like hell."

"Superb. It means all your ways are cleared. Hehehehe"

"Yup, dear, I just pray they accept Sunaina."

"Ok, now let's move to the office. Mr. Naveen must be searching for you."

"Yup, let's move now."

"Hi, Arjun; how are you, dude?"

Ankit called me up and asked me to come for *adda* at tea-stall.

"I am good, bro. What about you?"

"As usual, fit and fine. You say how the date was?"

"First, let's order tea. When are the others going to come?"

"Probably after half an hour."

"Why so late?"

"Do you want to share the details with others?"

"Yes"

"Oh, okay, then let's order and wait."

We waited an hour, and the gang started to show up slowly.

"Hi guys, sorry for being late," Vicky said.

"No worries, boy, we can understand your delay. What about you, Satyam?"

"Nothing much, but I had to accompany my parents to the temple. I guess I am also excused."

"Definitely, my saint," Ankit replied.

All of us exploded a vast laugh. After a long time, we were meeting like we used to. Someone indeed said – the time spent in your school and college is the best. You have no tension except your studies. I wish I could go back to that time.

"Where is Ritz?" I asked.

"He shall be coming in a minute," Vicky responded.

"Hi guys, order something for me, dude. I have been hungry since morning." Ritz took his spot.

We ordered tea and some snacks.

"Ok, guys, Arjun has got something to share."

"What's that? Did you get divorced from your online friend, too?" Vicky winked at me.

"Last night, I went on a date with Sunaina. I proposed to her."

The moment I finished, I could see the *mawaalipan* of my gang. They were whistling hard and dancing with joy.

"Wow, dude, congrats, buddy" Vicky was still in the mood to dance.

"Dumbass, first hear what she replied? That also matters." Ankit calmed them down.

"She, too, has the same feeling for me." Now, my group was uncontrollable. Sometimes, instead of getting angry in such situations, people laugh and thank God for blessing them with true friends. I was one of them.

"That's great news, buddy. By the way, tell us something about the date?"

I narrated the whole incident of our date on the Persian terrace.

"Wow, hot air balloon. Good job dude. That was the best part," Ankit said.

"Yes, dude, even she liked it a lot. I wish, just like me, my parents also accept her."

"No worries, dude. If they won't agree, we'll make them agree," Vicky said confidently.

"Sure, bro. So, how's it going with you and Shweta?"

"I guess you know better than me. You spend more time with her than I do," Vicky winked. *He was right.*

"It's a celebration time. Where is the party?" Ankit flashed the question.

"Wherever you guys say."

"A new pub has opened in Marathahalli. Let's go there." Vicky must have been working for Zomato. He knows everything about pubs even before they are famous.

"Ok, done. We shall meet on Sunday at 6.30 pm for drinks. Please be on time."

"No, dude, keep it on Saturday. I have to meet Shweta on Sunday. She said it was urgent."

"Urgent! Nice dude, you are on your way, I guess," I pinched.

"No, buddy, it's not like that. I find her a nice girl, and I prefer a long-term view rather than just short-term fun."

*I couldn't believe what he just said. But I felt relieved – at least he wouldn't be leaving her with a broken heart.*

"Ok, buddies, I need to go now. It's too late. My parents must be giving a missed call at any moment."

"It's tough to understand – You're such a miser; how come you afforded such an expensive date," Vicky asked.

"I realized – She was more valuable to me than some bucks. I wanted to make her feel special. And for that, if I needed to sell myself, I would have gone for it."

"Ok. Next time if you run out of money, come to me. I'll buy you," Ankit punched his wit.

"It would be my pleasure, buddy."

We laughed and laughed and laughed. It was probably the best laugh I had in a very long time. I felt so fresh and happy. I had everything I wanted.

By the time I reached home, it was already midnight. I was walking slowly towards my room. I was scared to face my mom at this moment. I was about to pass my parents' room when I heard some sobbing. My feet froze. I had never heard my dad crying or sobbing, and I was unable to move my feet.

I could hear my dad trying to say something but could not speak.

"Don't worry, things will get alright," my mom was consoling my dad.

I couldn't believe what I just heard. *Things would get alright. What does she mean by that? Has Dad got some problem? Has anything wrong happened in business? I was waiting for my dad to speak up.*

"I don't know how to come up from this trouble. I thought it would be a good investment idea, but things went wrong. My people deceived me. I have lost my money; my son is not there with me. I am feeling so helpless." My dad was still sobbing. I could feel his pain.

*I lost my money, and my son is not there with me. All these sentences were revolving in my head. He was in deep trouble. But why did he never open up about it to me? Did I fail to hear his calls? He always asked me to join him, but I always felt he was trying my strength. I wanted to go inside and check what was wrong, but before I could move, I heard him saying another hidden truth.*

"I thought it was a fair time to invest. I presumed that the market would touch its peak by the end of this month. I took a loan from my HNI friends and invested the money in the market. But due to some unassumed circumstances, the market fell on its face. The shares I bought are not going to fetch even a penny. I thought of getting some investors on board, but they also turned away at the last moment. I don't understand how to repay the loans?"

*I was shocked. Whatever the investment Dad made, it all sank. I never knew he played the gamble on loan money, too. I never saw him failing in the share market, but how did it happen today? I went past to his room, engulfed in the thought. I entered my room. It was dark. I rested my head on the pillow, but my mind was unrest. Suddenly, something buzzed under my pocket.*

"Hi, Arjun, you didn't call me up today. Is something wrong?" It was Sunaina.

"No way, sweetheart. I was busy with some stuff."

"What's the matter? I feel you're a bit tense. Tell me, dude, what happened to you?"

"Nothing dear. If you don't mind, can we please talk later? I need some rest. I apologize. Please don't take me wrong."

"Arjun, I can understand. It's ok if you want to rest. If you need my help at any point of time, I am there for you at any hour of the day. Take care. Good night. Sweet dreams. Love you"

"I love you too, sweetheart," and I hang the call. I closed my eyes so that I could catch some sleep.

When I got up, it was 8:30 a.m. I freshened up quickly. I reached the dining table. I could see only my aunt.

"Where are the rest?" I asked her.

"Your dad and uncle have gone to the office, saying they have some urgent work. Your mom has gone to the temple. For the rest of the members, you know where they would be," she replied.

"Ok, aunty. I'll leave now. See you in the evening." I took my last bite and left.

My heart was pumping hard. Evil thoughts were penetrating my mind and making it volatile. I was feeling weak in my legs. They were unable to move forward. The world seemed to be blank for me at the very moment. I started the ignition of my scooty and left.

In half an hour, I reached my dad's office. The security guard stood up and greeted me with wide-surprised eyes.

"Hello, Sir. Good Morning,"

"Good morning. Where is Dad?"

"He is in the office upstairs."

"Ok," and I left in a hurry.

I reached the floor where Dad's cabin was. From the glass wall, I could see him. He was looking towards the open window. His eyes were transfixed on the lake. It was calm. His hands reached the pocket and pulled out the kerchief to wipe his moist eyes. I couldn't stand there anymore.

"Dad, may I come in?"

He looked at me and stood still with shock on his face. Maybe he never expected me on his cabin's doorstep.

"Arjun," he could barely say my name.

"I heard you last night. Why didn't you tell me about this earlier?"

"I tried to say, but I felt you may get scared by the situation. I did not feel comfortable sharing my burden with you. I am sorry, Arjun."

"Don't be sorry, Dad. I never did anything extraordinary that can make you feel that I could share your burden."

After this, there was a long pause. Neither of us was in a position to say something. I went forward and took his hand in mine.

"Dad, don't worry. We will definitely find out some solution to get rid of this problem. It's only a matter of time. Today, the stocks are at low; tomorrow, they will gain."

"No one can say how volatile the market would react now. The stocks have gone to an all-time low. The amount I have lost is approximately 80% of my investment."

"No worries, Dad. We would surely come out of this menace soon. Have patience. I shall try to find out some ways."

My dad came forward and hugged me. It was the first time I felt his arms, and I always missed this moment. With moist eyes, I left his cabin. My mind was busy finding a way out when I was disturbed by a mobile ring. It was Sunaina.

"Hi dear, how are you?"

"I am good Sunaina. What about you?"

You're sounding so low. Is your health okay? Are you fine? Is something wrong, dear?"

I couldn't control myself, so I told Sunaina about everything.

"Oh no. How is he now? Is he fine?"

"Yeah, he is fine. But I don't understand how should I get him out of this trouble?"

"Dear, don't take tension. He needs your support. If you act as a tensed guy, how would he find solace?"

*Sunaina was right. I needed to be tough. All my life, my dad supported me. Now, the time has come to support him.*

"But Sunaina, I don't understand how to help him out of this. I mean, I have nil knowledge about the share market. As per him, the stocks have gone down to 80%. How should I help him regain the value and repay his loans?"

"Dear, you may help him in several other ways. You may not help him financially, but morally, you can. And believe me, moral help is much bigger than financial help."

"I didn't get you."

"Join his business and help him with day-to-day work. Once he starts believing your presence, he would gain the courage back, and you would see the problem is solved itself."

"How would it solve the problem?"

"If you join him and make him believe that you're there forever, he will start focusing his mind on earning money in different ways and paying back the debts. As far as I see, he is losing self-confidence. It is you who can restore it."

"But I have signed the bond with the company. I can't leave it for three years."

"Arjun, as I said earlier, remember your preferences. Who is more important to you now - Your dad or your job?"

"I guess you're right, dear. Thanks a lot for being with me and guiding me. I am lucky to choose you."

"Stop complimenting. I will see you later. Got to go. Love you"

"I love you too dear" and I hang the call with a soft kiss on the lower edge of my phone.

I have the solution to some extent. It was time to take the call—what did I need to do?

"Hi, dude, what's up?" It was Ankit.

"I am good, bro. What about you?"

"Have you forgotten about the day's plan?"

*I checked the calendar. It was Saturday. We had to meet in a pub.*

"Dude, I am stuck with something. I may not be able to make it today."

"Dude, I'm waiting for you downstairs. Come down soon, or I'll start honking."

"Dude, believe me. I shall not be able to come today."

"You're coming down, or shall I get the gang upstairs?"

"Bro, please try to understand..."

"I am sorry. I can't hear you. Either you come down, or I'll come up."

*Sometimes, it's really hard to make a friend understand. I gave up because I knew they wouldn't back out.*

"Ok, bro, just give me 10 minutes. I'll come down."

"Good for you," and he disconnected.

I reached down and saw my gang ready. We left for the pub.

In an hour, we reached the spot. It was a hut-shaped pub with lanterns hanging around the side. An escort dressed as a villager was standing at the door for checking. We went inside and took our seats. It was a microbrewery themed as a village in northern India. We settled down, and the waiter came up with the menu. As usual, Ankit placed our order. Meanwhile, I was looking around the ambiance. It had a small dance floor where some couple, probably drunk, were dancing their heart out. I saw a familiar face hiding behind a man's shoulder. Before I could rise, the waiter interrupted.

"Belgium beer for all of you. Anything to eat, sir?"

"Not right now. We shall order it later."

"Dude, just have a look at that girl. I think she is Shweta," Vicky whispered to me.

*Damn right. The familiar face was no one but Shweta. But what she was doing here with an unknown man (at least for us, he was unknown).*

"Yes. It is. But what is she doing here?"

Vicky decided to go and check it; meanwhile, we were sipping our beers and checking out for next. The very next moment, we saw Vicky leave the pub with anger on his face. We were unable to make out what had prompted him to run out like this. Ankit and others left to check out for Vicky, and I advanced towards Shweta to check what was wrong.

As I went near, I was stunned to see the man in the dim light. It was Mr. Naveen. I couldn't believe – He was with Shweta. *What was he doing here? Does it have to do anything with Shweta's past?*

Mr. Naveen decided to leave the place and left quickly. I took my seat near Shweta. Tears were rolling down her eyes. I put my hands on her shoulder. She broke down in tears. Everyone around us looked at me as if I were the reason for this.

"Calm down, Shweta. Would you please explain what had happened?"

"I told Vicky about my life's dark secret, and he could not digest it."

"What was the secret? And why Mr. Naveen was here with you?"

"Because he is the reason for my life's dark secret."

"What? I didn't get you. How is he related to all these things?"

"To secure a job and promotions, I had to compromise with Mr. Naveen several times. I came to this company for an interview and was rejected for the post. I was about to leave the place when Mr. Naveen saw me. He came to me and enquired about the purpose of my visit. I told him everything. He asked me to wait for a while and left. In a few minutes, the receptionist informed me that I should meet the AGM in the HR section. I went to his cabin and saw Mr. Naveen sitting there. I was told that I had been selected and asked to join the company asap. I was so happy to hear that I forgot to think about it – Why did Mr. Naveen interfere and secure a job for me? I started working at the company, and Mr. Naveen often called me for some excuse. Initially, I felt he was trying to help me, but it didn't take much time to face the reality.

One fine evening, Mr. Naveen called me up into his cabin and tried to touch me indecently. When I protested, he got angry. He told me harshly – either compromise, or you'll be fired. I was stunned to hear this. I left his cabin and decided to complain about him to my senior. When I approached him the very next day, I found Mr. Naveen was sitting with my senior. In front of him, he asked me about my decision. It was a shock for me. Even my senior was taking his side. I discussed it with one of my colleagues, who told me that Mr. Naveen uses every female staff member in his way. His sexual advances were growing every day. Financially, I was not a sound person. Things were getting more complicated for me. I tried to switch the job but failed. Finally, I gave up. I surrendered to Mr. Naveen. On the pretext of office meetings and tours, he would take me with him and do things to satisfy his sexual urges. I got pregnant sometime back, and he got it aborted and continued his harassment of me. When I met Vikram, I felt I might get a better life. But things spoiled when he faced the reality. I called Mr. Naveen to finish my chapter with him and tell Vicky everything about my past. But I guess I have lost him," She cried inconsolably.

*Whatever I just heard, I was unable to engulf it. She was a victim of sexual harassment in the office, and nobody dared to help her just because a moron was controlling the company. Simultaneously, I was deeply aghast to see my friend Vicky leaving her when she needed him the most. I was unable to understand Vicky's view. Why did he behave in such a silly way?*

I consoled Shweta and asked her to come along with me. We stepped out of the pub. It was getting darker, and I saw none of my gang members outside. We took the cab, and I went to drop Shweta off at her place.

# Chapter – 17

"Hi, Vicky," I dialled his number to discuss the evening matter.

"Hi, dude."

"May I know what had happened to you? Why did you leave the place?"

"Didn't she tell you anything? How could she do it?"

"Did you try to understand the reason behind her act?"

"Why should I?"

"Ok, tell me something. What had hurt you more – she wasn't a virgin, or she didn't tell you?"

"It doesn't matter. I never expected that she would sleep with someone for money. This is known as prostitution; you might know it."

"Shut up dude. I never expected that your mentality would go down so deep. Whatever she did, she did under pressure. She earns bread and butter for her family. I don't think you're so smart to understand how tough it is for a person when he chooses a path that is against his wish."

"Why you're taking her side?"

"Because she is my friend. I am more hurt to see your reaction. Instead of giving her your arms, you parted your ways. You said you're planning for a long-term relationship with her. Just because she slept with someone else, you think she is no more a human. To remind you, you also slept with several girls. Don't you think you have done wrong to their lives to satisfy your lust?"

*There was silence from both the end for a while. Maybe he was in two minds. Perhaps he was hurt to hear what I said.*

"Dude, I am sorry to say all this. But I wanted to make you understand that when you love someone, love their soul first, not their body. Shweta is a nice and decent girl. She told me earlier that she wants to share some dark secrets with you before she goes for the long term. But before this could happen, you met with the reality. You didn't let her explain the circumstances under which she made such a big decision."

"Dude, we should talk after some time?" Next, I heard a buzz.

"Hi, Sunaina; how are you?" I called her after reaching home.

"I am good, dear. How are you?"

"I am also good. Can I ask you something?"

"Of course, dear. Why do you need my permission?"

"Have we committed any mistake by making love that night?"

"Are you ok? Why are you asking this? Did somebody tell you anything?"

"No, dear. I just wanted to know your view."

"If you ask me, I don't think I made any mistake. I gave the most precious thing of my life to a person I love the most. For me, it was the moment when our souls united, where others may see it as an act of indecency."

"Why does our society blame a girl if she indulges physically but not the boy?"

"Dude, what happened to you? Why are you asking all this?"

*I told her everything that happened in the evening. I never knew that even a person's virginity also plays a vital role in a relationship. People always say love is an eternal feeling which unites two souls. When did this definition change from feeling to physical pleasure? Nobody knew.*

"I am sorry for your friend, but I guess Vicky would understand this and come back to her."

"I, too, hope for it. She told me earlier that before she plunges into a long-term relationship, she would share a dark secret with Vicky. I never knew that Vicky was too weak to digest her past. Even he slept with many girls, but never realized about his deeds in the past"

"It's ok. Let him take his time and understand the meaning of love. Then, I am pretty sure he would come back to Shweta."

"I, too hope so"

"Arjun, Can I ask you something?"

"Of course, dear. You may"

"Will your family accept me?"

"Certainly they will. Don't worry about it," I told her.

"What if they don't?" Sunaina asked.

"I'm sure I could convince them, dear. Take rest, dear. I shall call you tomorrow."

"Good Night, Dear," Sunaina said.

After the horrific past week, I was back to work. But I was unable to concentrate on it. I checked out for Shweta. She was busy with some interviews. I rested my bum on my chair again. As soon I started my laptop, things from the past week were notching on my head. My dad's crying face, Shweta, Vicky, Sunaina. I was finding it hard to concentrate anymore. So, I decided to move to the cafeteria. I was waiting for my coffee when my phone buzzed.

"Hello"

"Hi, Arjun," the female voice sounded very familiar. I checked the number again; *it was unknown.*

"Hello, may I know who this is?"

"It's Riya. How are you?"

"How come you called me?" *I know I should have said I'm fine, and I don't need you anymore, but her sudden call left me in awe.*

"I was missing you. How are you?"

"I'm good. How are you?"

"Without you, how can I be fine?"

*I must say it was a cheesy line. But apart from that, I could feel heaviness in her breathing. I felt as if she was crying and trying to control her tears from rolling down her cheeks.*

"Are you crying?"

"I can't believe it. You can still figure it out. Never knew you loved me so much."

*I had no other option but to listen. I was busy trying to determine the probable reason for her call.*

"How is your work going? Hope you're happy and satisfied!"

*The tone remained blank. She didn't respond to it. I was trying hard to avoid talking to her, but I was unable to do it. Why does your ex come back to you when you have already dived into another relationship?*

"Arjun, I am sorry for what I did in the past. I always chased fantasies, but I never realized your true love for me. I feel so low. I can imagine how much pain I had given to you. Would you ever forgive me?"

"Don't be sorry. Whatever happened in the past, let's bury it up there. How's your job going on?"

"Are you trying to avoid our relationship talk?"

"Dear, I don't know...."

"Please, Arjun, understand my situation. I never wanted to leave you, but circumstances led me to do it."

"I understand that, but..."

"But what, sweetheart?"

*Now, how do you cut the conversation when your ex is apologetic and calls you sweetheart? We guys are dumb.*

"Nothing Riya"

"Can we meet up for coffee someday?"

"I can't say about it."

"Please don't say no. I want to broom up our relationship from where I left it."

"Sure, dear. My boss is calling. I'll see you later." I had to make an *excuse.*

"No worries, honey. Let's plan for coffee. Message me whenever you're free. Love you dear. Take care"

"Bye, Riya," & I hung the call before she could say or ask me to say something.

*I recounted what had happened some moments ago. My ex called me up, and she was feeling apologetic. I realized all my anger toward her vanished as soon as I heard her voice. Do I still have feelings for her? I don't think so. I Love Sunaina, and only she deserves to be my Life Partner. Then, why is my mind crossed after talking to Riya? Why am I so confused?*

I checked Shweta's cabin during lunch. She was still in her cabin, focusing intensely on the file. But I knew where her mind was.

"Hi Dear, don't you want to have lunch today?"

"I am not feeling hungry, Arjun. Can we talk later?"

"How can I have lunch without you? Let's come up and have some bites." I took her hand in mine and forced her to leave the chair.

"Arjun, please leave me alone," the pitch was high. I could see the pain in her eyes. Her heart was in deep pain. Tears were soaked up in her eyes. I let her hands free. She broke into tears as she sat on the chair.

"I am sorry, Arjun. I don't know why I am unable to control myself. I miss him. How do I make him understand that whatever I did was not deliberate? It was my past. Can't he forget it and move ahead?"

"Tell me one thing – if you were in his place, what would you have done?"

"I would have given him a fair chance to explain his action. If he accepts his mistake and never commits it again, I would never desolate him."

"Hmmm...Just give him some time. I am sure he would understand his mistake and come back to you. After all, true love never faces defeat"

"Well said, but it's all bookish. I don't trust them anymore. I'll see you later. You have your lunch"

"If you don't accompany me, I won't have it"

"Please, Arjun, don't act like a kid."

"Please, Shweta, don't act like an adult." *Finally, I saw a light smile on her face since Saturday.*

"Let's come. I need some information from you."

"What information do you want?"

"First lunch, then chat." I forcefully took her off the seat, *and we left the cabin for lunch.*

"I swear I'll kill you if it is a joke," Ankit blasted as soon I told him what had happened in the morning.

"Dude, she called me up in the morning and was apologetic. I don't know what to say to her. I have already moved on with Sunaina, and now she has returned. Why did God never wish to see me happy?"

"You're really lucky, dude. Once upon a time, you had no girlfriend, and now you have options, and you're blaming God." Satyam took a sip.

"But did you ask her why she called you up after almost a year?" Ritz came up with something sensible.

"No, dude. I couldn't ask her. I was blank. I was finding it hard to talk. I don't know what to do now"

"Before you think what you want, think about it - what she wants." Satyam finished his tea.

*Finally, after a long time, I realised that even Satyam is a witty fellow. He was right. Why did she call me up? What did she really want?*

"But tell me, where is Vicky? There is no fun if Playboy is not there," Ritz asked.

"I have no idea. I called him, and he said he is busy in the office and won't be able to make it." Ankit shared the information.

"Strange. Now he started his playboy activities in the office too," Satyam said, making us laugh loud. I knew why he hadn't come.

"Let's move now. I may get a missed call from my mom anytime," Ritz said, finishing his tea.

We paid for tea and left for home. Ankit and I walked out of the stall together.

"Have you talked about Riya to Sunaina?"

"Yup, she knows about it."

"What do you think?"

"I Love Sunaina, but when I heard Riya crying over the phone and apologizing, my heart started melting."

"Dude, this time, I won't give you advice on what to do. Listen to your heart, and whomever you find good enough for you, go for it without a second thought."

"Thanks, dude. I know my decision," I winked at him.

"Are you going to Vicky's place?"

"Yeah"

"How do you know he is at home?"

"I know this because he has not gone to the office today."

"What? Then why did he lie to us?"

"Let's go and find this"

We reached Vicky's place in no time. The light in his bedroom was shut. We knocked at the door. Aunty opened the gate.

"Thank God you guys came. Did something wrong have happened? Vicky has not come out of his room since last day"

"Don't worry, Aunty. We would check it."

We proceeded towards his room. There was silence in the corridor. We entered his room without knocking and switched on the lights. Vicky was sitting at the corner of the bed with his head resting on the joints. He looked up to see. His eyes were red. One could easily make out that he was sobbing in the darkness. *Perhaps he was missing Shweta badly.*

"Hi, Buddy," we greeted in unison.

"Hi guys, sorry for not joining on tea"

"It's ok dude. We can understand your absence. I know you're missing Shweta. If you love her so much, then why don't you talk to her?"

"Arjun, do you think I should trust her again?"

"Yup, I truly think so. If you don't believe me, just hear this." I started a recording. It was mine and Shweta's recording, which I did when I went to her cabin.

After hearing it, Vicky was almost into tears. He broke down inconsolably.

"Will she ever forgive me for what I did to her?"

"You have heard it. So, I guess you know the answer. Just go to her and say whatever you have in your heart. It's better to be late than never."

"Ok, I shall meet her tomorrow. Thanks a ton, buddy. You saved me" Vicky hugged me.

"Any day, buddy," We bid good night and left for our house.

"Hi, sweetheart, how are you?"

"Thanks, Mr. Arjun. You called up. I thought you had forgotten me." This is how Sunaina sounds when she is angry.

"I know you're angry with me, and I apologize. I am sorry"

"It's ok. Where have you been for the day?"

"Finally, I got the love birds united. Vicky will meet Shweta tomorrow."

"Oh, that's great. Good going dude. But how did it happen?"

*I narrated the entire thing to her.*

"Oh, so Mr. Arjun knows how to do a recording too. I hope your phone was not on recording that night"

"Who knows? But I would say you were looking very beautiful that night"

"Shut up," we both giggled.

"How was your day?" I enquired.

"Day was fine. My project would be over in the next seven days. I wanted to talk to my parents about you, but I feel very nervous. I don't know how to tell them?"

"Just tell them about me. Tell them everything you know about me. I hope they will accept me"

"Yeah, I should tell them everything. Let's start like this. You had a girlfriend in the past. You're witty. You have good looks. You treat me in a special way. You're good in..."

"You're good in..." *I knew what she wanted to say, but you hardly let a chance go when you can pull the legs of your lover.*

"Leave it. Tell me, have you thought about how you'll recover the losses of your father?"

"I have got no idea. I don't know how to sort out this issue. Have you got something on this?"

"Last day I spoke to my dad on this. He said there was no way, but you had to pay back the amount you had taken. It's on your luck if those stocks take a sudden turnaround"

"You told your dad about me?"

"No, dumbo. I said one of my friend's father had faced this problem. Accordingly, he replied to it. Arjun, what if your family doesn't accept me?"

"It would never happen. You're so pretty and classy that no one can think of rejecting you"

"Riya also had a class and was prettier than me. Then why was she rejected?"

*I could sense insecurity in her mind. I have never heard her so perplexed. She had a valid point to panic. Why did my family reject Riya even though she was prettier than Sunaina? Perhaps I never tried to find the depth of the rejection. I just accepted what my mom said – She doesn't have a class, she won't be able to adjust to our traditional values, etc. Did we love each other, or was it just our fancy that we were in love? I don't think so. I loved her from the bottom of my heart. I cried and cried and cried when she left me deserted.*

"Arjun, are you there?"

"Yeah, baby."

"You didn't answer me – why she was rejected? She was rejected merely because she wanted to do the job, or something else was the reason?"

"My family believes in traditional values, and Riya was exactly the opposite. She belongs to the modern era, where she feels she can make decisions about her life and lifestyle. She never cared if her decision impacted someone else's life, too. Probably, this was the reason which made my family uncomfortable about her"

"Do you think I don't belong to that same genre of Riya?"

"No, you don't. You care for my family; you care for me. And I know you would never take a step that can harm anyone's interest"

"Oh, So Mr. Arjun knows me that well."

"Yeah, sweetheart. I know you very well. Let's meet tomorrow evening"

"Sure. But I won't be able to come for a long hour. I have some deadlines to meet. Can you come to my hotel?"

"So sweet of you. I like the invitation," I giggled.

"Men will always remain Men. Can you ever think from your heart as well?"

*This time, we both giggled. I always enjoy that sweet rhythm of her giggling. Every time she smiles, I thank God for choosing her for me.*

"I need to go now. I'll see you later"

"Sure, honey. I'll see you later. Love you baby"

"Love you too, honey. Muah. Bye," And she disconnected the call.

# Chapter – 18

I reached my office on time. I could see a pile of files on my desk. I took a deep breath and entered the war zone by switching on the laptop, which sounded similar to a conch shell to begin the day. From the corner of my eye, I saw Shweta coming towards me.

"Hi, Arjun, can I have a minute with you?" and she walked towards the AV room. My colleagues were looking at me as if there was some good news.

I went inside the room and closed it.

"Hi Shweta, good morning"

"Hi, Arjun. Good morning."

We were silent for a while, not knowing what to say. Finally, Shweta broke the ice.

"I don't find words how to thank you. I felt I had lost Vicky, but you tried, and I got him back. I will never forget this deed of yours. Thanks a ton for bringing my love back."

"Don't be silly. You both loved each other, and it was the strength of your love that brought you guys back together. I haven't done anything, dear. By the way, what he said?"

"He told me everything. How you recorded my feelings and played in front of him. All I can say is thanks a lot for doing it. He asked me if I could meet him and talk about what spoiled our relationship for a while."

"Great. Good going, dear."

"You say how Sunaina is?"

"She is fine. She will be returning back to Mumbai next week."

"You don't feel like fine. Is there any problem?"

"Buddy, I want to introduce her to my family and talk about the things. But I don't know how my family will accept it. Moreover..."

"Moreover, what?"

"Last day, my ex called me up and wanted to patch up"

"Why does she want to patch up now? Just because you did what she wanted you to do?"

"I have no idea. She wanted to meet me. I am feeling uncomfortable. In movies, it's really simple to choose one in a love triangle, but when the same situation arises in your real life, you get perplexed."

"Why you're getting perplexed? Do you still have a soft corner for Riya?"

"Not really, but I feel like I am trapped between Sunaina and Riya. I know I love Sunaina very much and want her to be my life partner, but don't know why something is trapping me."

"When you know and want Sunaina to be your life partner, what's the issue?"

"If I had any idea, I would have sorted the issue myself, dear."

"Look, I can understand you're still attached to Riya emotionally, but you need to understand life needs some aspect of practicality apart from emotions"

"I know, dear, but I am finding it hard to tell Riya that I have moved on and chosen Sunaina as my life partner."

"You know your problem; you're still emotionally attached to Riya. Maybe you hate her die-hard, but somewhere in your heart, you have a soft corner for her. You can't see her crying when you tell her about the rejection. Am I right?"

"Probably. Who can see a girl crying?"

"Did she care for you when she took the decision to move out of the relationship?"

"Nope. She hinted that she wants to move out of the relationship."

"I don't think it's hard for you to understand that she never cared for you. All she cared was she."

"Maybe. Let's get back to work. Will see you at lunch hour."

"Sure, Arjun. I have some more things to talk about with you. Let's meet tomorrow. Today, I shall leave on half a day."

"As you say. Take care. I will see you another day." I left the chamber.

I reached my workstation and took a glance at the pile. I started working on one of the files, but my mind wandered elsewhere. I was unable to concentrate. Sometimes, you find yourself in a situation where you have options; you know what to choose, but still, you feel bad for rejecting the other. I looked around. Everyone was lost in their work. I wanted to get rid of the place right away, but corporates have some norms that you are coerced to follow. I was waiting for the watch to tickle at 1. Without interest, I started looking into files when my phone buzzed.

"Hi, Riya."

"Hi Arjun, how are you?"

"I am good. How are you?"

"Good as usual. Can we meet today if you're free?"

"I don't think so. I am loaded with a huge pile of files. All of them are urgent and relate to sub-contractors. Can we meet some other day?"

"Sure. We shall meet some other day. Arjun, do you still love me?"

"I'll call you back. My boss is calling me. Bye, take care, dear," and disconnected before hearing a word from her.

*Sometimes, even a monster can be your saviour.*

I cast my eyes back to the pile once again and took one from it. Uninterestingly, I started working on it. People around me started moving out with their Tiffin, which made me realize that half the day was over. I packed my laptop and other accessories and moved out before anyone could ask me anything.

"Dad, I need to talk about something with you." I was standing in my dad's chamber. I thought I needed to clear the mess in my life ASAP.

"About what Arjun?"

"I had spoken to one of my friends who works for loan syndication. He said that by looking at your creditability and business stocks, banks can give you a loan. With this loan, we can pay back our debts to lenders. One more thing, I have decided to work with you now"

*My dad's eyes were wide open once he heard the last sentence. Probably, he wasn't expecting this to come out.*

"Are you sure you want to do this?"

"Yes, Dad."

"But why all of a sudden you want to join me?"

*Now, this is what irritates me. At first, they wanted me to join the business, and when I wanted to join it, they wanted to know the motive and reason behind it.*

"So that next time you don't make such a loss-making investment," we laughed hard.

I went near to him and hugged him.

"It makes me so happy that my son is with me now. Now, my strength shall be double. But tell me one thing, how would you join me? You have signed a contract with your company."

"I'll manage that, Dad. Don't worry about it."

"I can't believe what I just heard. If you have any wishes, tell me, and I'll fulfil them."

"Not now, Dad. I'll tell you when the suitable time comes."

"Sure, son. Would you like to have something to eat?"

"No, Dad. I have to go somewhere. I'll see you later."

"Sure, Arjun."

"Hi, Sunaina." I was almost ten minutes late to meet her in the restaurant.

"Hi honey, how are you?" She was looking fabulous as usual.

"I am good. How are you?"

"As usual, fine."

"So, you're leaving next week?"

"Yup."

"What have you decided?"

"About what?"

"About our future."

"It's bright, and we'll have two kids," she giggled hard. I also couldn't stop my laugh.

"I want to marry you, but before that, I want to finish my course and start a boutique on my own and…"

"And what?"

"I want you to decide your future course of action regarding your job."

"I have decided."

"What?"

"I shall join my dad's business. I guess he needs me more than any other corporate."

"Really? It's a nice decision, honey."

"Thanks, Sunaina."

"I guess it's the first time you decided firmly."

"Why? I guess it's the second. The first one was my proposal to you."

"You proposed to me, but you still have something to decide. Arjun, I won't force you to make any decision in haste, but whatever you decide, stay with it till the end."

*Sunaina was right. I always get nervous before making any decision. In life, we are usually left with two options. Then, why do we feel so uncomfortable choosing the best among them? Why, when things are going smoothly, am I making it more complicated?*

"Arjun, if you have anything to discuss, you can bring it on."

"Nothing like that, Sunaina. I am just sad that you'll be leaving from here by next week."

"Well tried, Arjun, but waste. I won't force you to disclose what you're hiding. But if you can share it with me, I am here to hear you out. I need to go now. Bye, Arjun."

"Please don't go," I held her hand and requested a seat.

"Arjun, the day you start sharing all your problems with me, I'll sit beside you. Take care, Bye," and she left.

*I won't say she was harsh towards me. She did what any person would do. It was my time to decide for which I shall not repent.*

I came home and marched straight towards my room. I fell on my bed with my eyes semi-closed, thinking about what had happened in the restaurant. Suddenly, I felt something vibrating beneath me. I took a look. Shruti was on the other side.

"Hi, Shruti."

"Hi, Arjun," I could feel she was sobbing.

"Hey, shrutz, what happened dear? Why you're crying? Did anybody say anything?"

"Nobody said anything, Arjun. How are you?"

"Shrutz, I am not feeling good about it. Something is wrong with you. You know you can't hide things from me. So, tell me, what has happened?"

"He ditched me."

"What are you saying? Why did he ditch you?"

"Simple – he lost interest in me."

"Lost interest in you? What do you mean by it?"

"He completed his MBA and wanted to return to India. I asked him to wait here for some more time. Then, we would go together and inform our parents about our relationship."

"Then what?"

"He said that our horoscopes do not match and his family won't let him get married to me. I tried to convince him many times, but he didn't bother. A day later, my roommate said she saw him getting into a pub with one of his classmates. I went down there, and what I saw was pathetic. He was inappropriately holding her and kissing her bare skin. He didn't notice that I was watching all these things. He crossed all his limits on that couch, and I could do nothing except watch it," and she cried inconsolably. I could feel her pain. She was deeply in love with the guy, and that cheap, mean guy ditched her once his purpose was solved.

"I have decided to return to India."

"Why dear? You went there to make your career..."

"What career, Arjun? The person for whom I was doing everything has left me. We had many dreams to fulfil, but those were only my dreams. He just wanted to satisfy his urge. I feel so cheated. You were right, Arjun; although I was living in London, my roots belonged to India. I should not have let go of my dignity."

"Just forget the past. Don't you see it was his loss? He left such a pretty and intelligent girl who loved him the most in her life. It was never your mistake because whatever you did was for his happiness. And whatever he did with you, he will repay for it someday."

"It's ok, Arjun. I have already decided that I am moving back to India..."

"And what excuse will you put up when your dad asks why you want to leave it in the middle?"

"I have no idea. I am just unable to concentrate on anything. I feel so lost. Don't know what to do?"

"Dear, why do you feel you're alone? Don't you think we all are there for you? Don't give up. I know it's your worst time, but believe me, you have the potential to overcome it."

"You can say it comfortably now, but tell me one thing, will you say the same if Sunaina remains no more in your life?"

*For a moment, I was numb. I can't imagine how my life would be if Sunaina left me!*

"Sorry, Arjun, if you're hurt, but I didn't mean it. Stay happy with Sunaina forever. By the way, how is she?"

"She is fine. Next week, her project is getting completed, and she will be leaving for Mumbai."

"What are you waiting for? Talk to Uncle and Aunty about her, and I am sure they would agree to your choice this time."

"I know, but...."

"But what dumbo?"

"I am in the midst of confusion."

"You always have confusion. Tell me, what's new this time? Aren't you sure you want to go for Sunaina?"

"Riya wants to come back."

*The next moment, all I could hear was a devil's laugh. Shruti was laughing without understanding my situation, and I felt like an idiot.*

"You're such a dolt. You think that's confusion. It's so simple, Arjun. Why do you find it so difficult?"

"Because I can't see anyone hurt."

"So you want to marry both?" *I know it was sarcasm.*

"No duffer. I feel bad to find myself in between them."

"Why do you feel bad? You're the luckiest guy. Two girls are dying to be with you."

"And I am dying only for one."

"Then, choose the one whom you're dying for."

*The answer was correct and straightforward.*

"Arjun, don't depend on someone else's advice. Ask your heart who can make your life better? Who can bring happiness in your life?"

"I know whom I need to choose, but..."

"Arjun, you can't keep everyone happy with one decision. Any one of them would be hurt and you need to be strong enough to handle it. It's good to see that you care for Riya, even though she had hurt you in past.

But it's about your life. You have to make a wise decision"

"Thanks Shruti. I always knew you're my saviour. Just message me the whereabouts of Akash"

"Why you want it?"

"Just want to send you a pic of him with blue eyes, red nose and white bandage over his head"

"Lol. No need of it. As you said, it was his loss to leave me, so I believe that"

"True and this time I have got no confusion about it"

*We both laughed and I bid a bye to Shruti and hang the call.*

◆

# Chapter – 19

"Hi, dude, what's up?" *Ankit always calls at odd hours. This time, it was 11:56 p.m.*

"Hi Ankit, how are you?"

"I am good, what about you? How is Sunaina *Bhabhi?*"

"She is good. Her project is over, and she will leave by next week."

"Then what are you waiting for, idiot? You're not a Shahrukh Khan for whom Kajol would come running."

"I know Ankit, but I don't know how to talk about her with Mom and Dad."

"Arjun, why are you so confused and stressed? Why do you need someone else's hand to help you all the time?"

"I know Ankit. Everybody has the same complaint with me."

"If you know everybody is unhappy with it, why don't you change it?"

"Buddy, I don't know why I feel so confused when making a firm decision."

"It's because you lack self-confidence, buddy. Just believe in your abilities, and things will be alright."

"I guess you're right. Thanks, buddy. Now I'll take my decisions on me. Let some of them be wrong, but now I will do what I want."

"Great. I hope it remains the same till morning also."

"Till morning, what you mean by that?"

"A guy feels he can conquer the whole world at night only. By morning, he realises his position."

"Hahahaha, quite funny. But mark my words, I'll make my decisions and will follow them."

"Hope it happens. What about Vicky? Is he fine now?"

"Yup, doing well. They are back together."

"It's a nice dude. Finally, our Casanova got his love of life."

"Yeah, man, but what about you?"

"Will speak to Sunaina and check if she has a younger sis or cousin."

*We both let out a monstrous laugh that could shake anybody.*

"Ok, dude, now I need to go. I will catch you soon."

"Sure, Ankit, see you; Bye, bro," and I hang the call.

*Someone truly said that if you want to know a person's nature, talk to his friends. Only they can tell you what he is when he is alone. Now, it was time for action, and I knew exactly what I needed to do next. I was eagerly waiting for the morning to arrive.*

Long awaited morning arrived. I was getting ready for office. My heart was beating fast, but somehow, I calmed myself by keeping my hands on my heart and saying All is Well. All thanks to "Three Idiots". I reached the office in less than half an hour. I walked straight to Mr. Naveen's cabin. The Old monk rested his bum on his seat and his head on the table. It seems like he was kicked out of the home and slept here last night. Poor Soul!

"Mr. Naveen, I would like to speak with you if you don't mind." I tried to wake him up with a slight push from my fingers.

He woke up as if he had been punched hard.

"What happened? And how come you came so early today?"

The monster left his seat and went to the washroom to refresh himself. Ten minutes later, he came back, looking fresh and innocent.

"Tell me what you have got to say today?"

"I want to put my papers"

For a moment, he felt I was kidding.

"Arjun, have you forgotten about the contract? Do I need..."

"No, Mr. Naveen, I remember everything. I know the terms and conditions of my job, but did someone tell you that you might get kicked out of your house tonight if you create a problem for me or Shweta?"

*The monster lost his innocence. He was looking red, more than the apples of Shimla.*

"Mind your words, Arjun. Who you think of yourself to kick me out of my house?"

"Who said I'll kick you out? It would be your wife to kick you out of the house."

*Mr. Naveen looked perplexed. He didn't understand what I was talking about.*

"I have got some pics of yours and other girls, which are inappropriate for a person having a wife."

"So, you're blackmailing me?"

"Nopes. I am here to make a deal. You give me farewell from the office without any problem, and I'll give you away your pics."

"What's the guarantee that you'll not play foul?"

"For your information, as per our CA institute guidelines and recent case law, a man had to lose his CA degree when he was caught in such an indecency act. Moreover, his wife got divorced easily, and today, she is enjoying 50% of her ex-husband's wealth. I guess you have got my point now."

*Even in the calm atmosphere, the monster was perspiring. He took out his kerchief to wipe the sweat from his head.*

"Before I grant acceptance to your resignation letter, I want to see those pics."

"Sure, I have got hard as well as soft copies for you. Have a look at these printed memories of yours?"

I handed him an envelope, and he started checking out one after another. He was sweating profusely, and he was constantly looking at me and those photographs.

"When do you want your termination letter?"

"I want it today, along with my settlement cheque."

"It's not possible. You can't..."

"Mr. Naveen, I won't mind losing a few bucks, but would you like to lose your membership, house, and respect?"

*The monster has no answer. He was in a situation of check-and-mate.*

"I want things to be closed and cleared by today. Before I leave the office at 5.00 pm, I need the settlement cheque and the acceptance of the resignation letter for both me and Shweta."

*I never knew I could be so good at handling a monster.*

"Ok, you'll get it. But I want the entire set of pics."

"You'll get the pen drive once I get my desired things."

*I left the cabin with a bang. When I reached my seat, an email appeared under Mr. Naveen's name.*

*It was an announcement that I was quitting the job due to family reasons, and asked the HR department to clear my dues ASAP.*

As soon as I finished reading the emails, I saw Shweta standing beside me.

"What's this dude? How did he accept our resignation so easily? Why did he ask the HR department to clear our dues so easily? I feel something is fishy."

"Did you remember a few days back when I asked you to provide me with some information about Mr. Naveen's affair, and you provided me with the information?"

"Yeah, I remembered."

"I hired a professional detective and asked him to click some pics of Mr. Naveen and other girls. Yesterday I received the parcel. I threatened Mr. Naveen to share these pics with the CA institute and his wife if he denies my demands. He agreed to whatever I have demanded. By evening, we will get our farewell and our final settlement amount, too."

"You have really turned bad," Shweta winked at me.

"After all, he tried to ruin the relationship of my sis-in-law," I winked back.

We kept on chatting while my colleagues took their seats. Suddenly, I saw Padmini come running towards me.

"You're resigning so early. It's not even a year you've completed. Is anything wrong?"

"Nothing wrong, Padmini *ji*. I have decided to help my dad in his business and take care of his financials."

Meanwhile, Atul, Mani, and Suresh also occupied chairs near my workstations.

"Tell me, Arjun, did you have a fight with Mr. Naveen?"

"Nopes. Why do you feel like this?"

"I went to his cabin for some correction in the vendor's agreement this morning, and his face looked dull. When I came to my workstation, I saw a mail stating that you have resigned, and it is accepted with effect from today," Suresh asked.

"Nothing is wrong, Suresh *ji*. I made him understand my scenario, and he accepted it."

"We will miss a jovial guy who changed the way and atmosphere of working in our company. Turned a monster into a humble, helping senior." Of course, *Padmini was talking about Sharath.*

"Let's forget the past, Padmini *ji*. Now, he is a man with a changed heart. Let's support him and seek his help whenever needed," I said.

From the corner of my eye, I saw Sharath walking towards my workstation with heavy steps.

"Arjun, you're leaving the company, and Shweta is also leaving. What's the matter?"

"Nothing, Sharath; I am leaving my job to help my dad in his business."

"And I am leaving my job since I got one in another company. They are paying more than my expectations," Shweta replied.

"We wish both of you all the very best. You two have been good buddies since Arjun joined the company. May you guys stay happy forever."

*It was Atul this time. We couldn't stop our laugh. I never knew people were thinking of me and Shweta in a relationship. It's so weird; you're linked with a girl who is your friend. And here is why this proverb stays right – A boy and a girl can't be friends.*

"You're wrong dude. We're just friends. She is committed to someone else."

"Oh, is it so? I am really sorry."

"It's ok Atul. We have some formalities to complete. We'll see you guys later."

"Definitely, but before you leave, we need a party from you."

"Oh, is it so? I thought you guys would give me a send-off party."

"We'll give it in office, but later, you'll have to give us a party."

"Done. This evening, we'll party."

*The mob dispersed, and we went to the HR head cabin.*

"Hi, Arjun; I received an email from Mr. Naveen. Tell me, how come you convinced him so easily to clear off your dues? You were under contract with the company."

"I was, but now I am not. Mr. Naveen understood my situation and co-operated with me in this regard."

"I don't know what to say, but I'm sad that you'll be leaving us soon. Mr. Naveen always said you're an important asset to our company."

"Even I regret leaving such a huge brand, but one can't have all the flavours in life."

"Yeah, true. No worries, Arjun. I'll clear your dues by noon. Some formalities need to be done regarding your relieve, and we shall complete them by evening. I wish you all the best for your plans."

"Sure, sir, I'll take your leave. Thanks a lot for your wishes."

"You're welcome, Arjun. Shweta, stay here for a while. I have some important work to discuss with you."

"Sure, sir." Shweta stayed in the cabin, and I left.

*It was an incredible feeling. On your last day in the office, there was no work pressure, and people said so many good things on your face, which they hardly said when you were in the organization. The last day makes you nostalgic. Let it be your last day in school, college, or the office. From the distance, I saw Sharath in the corridor. Maybe he was also searching for me. I went near to him.*

"Hi Sharath, how are you?"

"Hi, Arjun, I am good; how are you?"

"I am good. Sorry I couldn't inform you about my resignation earlier."

"It's ok dude. I can understand. I wish you all the best for your future endeavours."

"Thanks a lot, Sharath. Keep in touch."

"Definitely. If you need any help from my end, feel free to contact me at any point of time."

"Thanks Sharath. I'll surely do that."

"Ok, Arjun, enjoy your last day. But give me a favour. Kindly hand over the task that you have been working on so that I can delegate it to someone else."

"I'll do that. I have already made a folder on my laptop along with workings and notes. I shall give it as and when you're free."

"That's great, Arjun. Seems you had planned your exit way earlier. Anyway, I'll take a leave now. We will meet after lunch for the handover task."

"Sure, Sharath, I'll be there." With this, Sharath passed beyond me.

*I had done what I wanted to do, but now two things were in front of me to finish, and I knew exactly how to do them. I took my cell phone, dialled a number, and fixed the meeting at 7.30 pm sharp. I wanted things to move smoothly.*

"Hi, Arjun. Let's go out for lunch. I guess it would be the last time we will be having lunch together."

"Nope, I don't think so. As long you are connected with Vicky, we can have lunch any day, *Bhabhi*."

'Yo, *Devar ji*," we busted into laughter.

"Let's go, Shweta Bhabhi," *we walked towards the company's gates.*

We reached our favourite dining place and ordered *regular thali*.

"Tell me something, what's your next plan? I am pretty sure you'll not leave Mr. Naveen so easily."

"You'll see it in a few days. Trust me"

'Ok. How's Sunaina?"

"She is good. But I guess she is upset with me."

"Why? What have you done now?"

"I am unable to give her my time. I have some big plans for our future, but I am stuck in these petty things. You know, only two days remain for her to return to Mumbai."

"What are your big plans? And what's running into your mind?"

"I want to introduce her to my family. Dad won't have any problem, but I am worried about my mom. God knows how she would react to my choice."

"Don't worry. I am sure this time she would accept your choice."

"Let's see. When are you guys planning to tie the knot?"

"We both are focusing on our careers. We may plan for marriage after two years."

"Great. So you have got two years' time to think upon"

"Hahaha, very funny."

"So, what are your plans as of now?"

"I have forwarded my resume to a few companies. Let's see if I get any luck."

"Why don't you work in my company? I mean my family business."

"Thanks for the offer, Arjun, but I guess this time I want to do it with my talent, not with any help. I hope you won't feel bad about it."

"Not at all. Vicky is so lucky to have you."

"We both are thankful to you. It was you who brought us together from the bad times."

"Chuck it, dear. Now eat fast. We have a send-off party awaiting."

"True dear. I wish they get some good quality cake."

We finished our lunch and moved back to our office. When we reached, we saw our colleagues were waiting for us with bouquets and some gifts in their hands. The VC room was turned into a mini party hall. A two-tower cake was waiting to be sliced by us. The room was scented with room spray. We were invited near to the cake. A message was crafted over the top of the cake: - *We wish you hearty success to both of you. We are sad to bid you goodbye, but you guys will always be there in our hearts.* For a moment, I was speechless.

"Before we begin the celebration, I would like to invite Mr. Naveen and say a few words about the duo." Sharath was the coordinator.

A way was cleared and Mr. Naveen came towards the table. With his look, one could say he was petrified.

"Good afternoon to all. Honestly, I find no reason to celebrate today. We are losing two precious assets who have a lot for the company. Firstly, I would say something about Shweta. She was a hard-working girl. She never said no to any work that came her way. She was modest and helpful. She was a very sincere HR manager. Thanks for your valuable services. I wish you luck for your future from the bottom of my heart."

"Thank you, Mr. Naveen," Shweta replied.

"Now, I would say something about Arjun. When I first met him on campus, I knew this guy had fire in him, and he would do anything to mark his presence. He fought all the odds. He taught people to work together and help each other without any greed. I had never heard Sharath appreciating someone so much. I guess you're the first and the last on this list, Arjun. I wish you all the best for your future plans. I know your dad needs you more than us, and hence, I, on behalf of the company, terminated your agreement as of today." *The last line won my heart.*

"Thanks a lot, Sir, for understanding."

"You're welcome, Arjun."

"Now, I would like to invite Shweta to say something."

Shweta went near the corner of the oval-shaped table.

"The journey wouldn't have been easy without you guys. My seniors and juniors supported me as and when

I needed them. I am lucky to have the tag Ajnara Constructions on my resume. During my journey, I made many friends and lost a few of them. Ajnara taught me to keep calm even if you're not having the perfect time. I thank all my friends here for being with me throughout the time. Thanks to everyone."

"That's pretty good, Shweta. Even we are also losing a sweet and good-looking HR manager." No one expected this to come from Sharath. We laughed hard.

"Now I'll call the boy of the hour, Arjun."

"Good Afternoon to all of you. Before I proceed, I would like to say thank you. Thank you for giving me your support and help as and when required. I joined this company merely a year ago. I had no idea how real estate companies function. I faced a lot of troubles. Many things were new to me that I never learned, or I would say I never got that chance. Slowly, things began taking the desirable shape. I started getting into the system more and more. All thanks to Mr. Naveen, who showed confidence in me and raised the bar of criticalness every time. Sharath helped me and guided me through such criticalness. Last but not least, I would like to thank my Accounts team – Mani, Atul, Suresh, and Padmini. Without your support, I was nothing. I thank all of you from the bottom of my heart."

The loud noise of claps followed by the end of my speech. It continued for a minute or two.

"Now I would like to invite both Shweta and Arjun to come and cut the cake," he said, giving Shweta a nicely worn ribbon knife.

*Shweta started cutting the cake, and the room was filled with claps. She took the first piece and put it in Sharath's mouth. The guy must be feeling lucky today. Then, I took a slice and rubbed the piece gently over her face. She took her turn and started doing it over my face. I turned my head to see, but Mr. Naveen was not there. The celebration continued for a while, and we all headed towards the washrooms. After cleaning, we returned to our desks. I saw a card on my desk which read – Come to my cabin, Mr. Naveen here.*

I went to his cabin and locked the doors.

"Arjun, here is your final settlement money. You'll get the PF amount after two months. I'll take care of those formalities. Shweta's final settlement has been given to her. Now, I have a few questions for you. Why did you do this to me?"

"You ruined so many lives for your lust. You should be thankful that I haven't beat you to the pulp. I had two motives behind this. One you know, I want to join my family business to support my dad. The other is you took undue advantage of my would-be sister-in-law."

"Sister-in-law?

"Yup, Shweta is my would-be sister-in-law. And dare not to play with the life of any other girl, else you'll face me again. Oh, by the way, I almost forgot to tell you. The courier has been despatched to your house."

"What courier?"

"Your love life outside the marriage pics have been sent to your wife."

"You double-crossed me. You son of a...."

"Shut up, you moron. Dare not you speak a word ahead of it. Today is my last day, and tomorrow it will be yours. So enjoy your last day. One more thing: never try to cross my path of my sister-in-law's path. You'll see the worst coming." With this, I bolted the door hard in his face.

*My heart skipped a beat—how did I manage to do so? My eyes were still on fire. My mind tried to calm me down, but I was unable to. I took my final settlement cheque and left. Downstairs, I saw Shweta.*

"Hi Shweta, you didn't go?"

"I was waiting for you. All the best. I know what you're going to do next. Trust me, it's the right thing you're doing."

"Really?"

"Yup. Now, don't waste time. I'll catch you later."

I ignited my scooty engine and rode towards the next mission.

# Chapter – 20

"Hi Riya, how are you?" I was on time for a change.

"Hi, Arjun; it's good to see you after a long time. Moreover, you're on time. That's really nice of you." She looked as pretty as she used to look.

"How are you? How are things going at your end?"

"Going well. Let's order something before we start talking." She smiled and took the menu card. A waiter took his place near her and started noting the order. All this time, I was trying to find a way - how to start and finish the conversation/

"Arjun, you're alright?" she enquired.

"Yeah, I am fine. You say, how is your office life going on?"

"Going great. You know, just in less than a year, I got more than 20 proposals. People are so mad about me." *She had a broad smile on her face. I felt she was trying to make a note – Don't you think Arjun, you're the only rich guy; many others are waiting in the queue.*

"But somewhere, I knew I could never get true love from them. Now that you're working, we can build our relationship again," she said, placing her palms on my hand.

"I left my job."

"What? Are you kidding? Is it a joke?" she was perplexed.

"Nope. It's not. I quit my job to join my family business. My dad needs me more"

"Arjun, you left such a big brand for such a silly reason?"

"Probably it is a silly reason for you, just like for me it was silly to take up a job to avenge you. All this time, I always thought that I'd show you my capabilities, but I ignored my dad and his wishes. He wanted me to join his business, but I behaved like a silly kid. I denied him. I got a job and started working. Then I realized that more than this company, my dad needs me. Silly when you left me because you thought I was not capable of taking care of you, your dreams. You can never imagine how hard I cried under the blankets at night. Even in the crowd, I felt lonely without you. Then, I found a companion who helped me in all possible ways without even asking for anything in return. I love her, and I'll marry her." *When I finished, I saw droplets of tears rolling down her cheeks. She was trying hard to stop them.*

"It means..." she choked.

"It means we can never be together. We had good memories. Let's finish this on a good note. I am sorry if

I have hurt you, but this is what I have got to say tonight. I love someone else"

"It's okay, Arjun. It was my mistake. I compromised love with my ambitions, for which I am paying the price now." She was unable to speak anything further. She took the napkin and wiped her eyes.

"I am sorry, Riya. I know you're hurt. Please forgive me for hurting you. I would love it if you accepted my friendship for life." I said.

"Do you think it would be easy for me to stay as friend with you?"

"I know it's not easy. I remember once you also asked me to be your friend after our break-up, but I couldn't accept it because I knew I would never be able to treat you as my friend. But I would request you to be my friend"

"I don't know Arjun, but I'll try," she said, wiping the last droplet from her cheek.

"We shall be friends forever. And I wish you all the best for your future. May God bless you with the entire world's happiness," I said.

"Thanks, Arjun. I also wish you happiness and prosperity in your life." We smiled.

"Let's have the food. It smells so delicious." I moved my hands towards my plate.

"Yup. Also, tell me about your life partner?"

We kept munching, smiling, and sharing what was happening in our lives. It was a sigh of relief that things didn't go wrong. Now I knew my last task.

It was a bright morning, and intense sunlight interrupted my sleep. I checked the time on my mobile. It was 8:21, and three calls from Shweta. I called her back.

"Hi Shweta, what happened? You called me up so early in the morning?"

"Did you hear something? Police have arrested Mr. Naveen."

"That's great. Finally, the sexaholic will have a good time behind bars"

"And it may surprise you, his wife filed a complaint about him"

"Nope, it's not a surprise for me. I sent her the pictures along with a note saying that Mr. Naveen indulges in affairs with many office colleagues. Only you can save these girls from his evil intentions"

"I can't believe it; you just screwed the monster," we both laughed.

"So Sunaina is leaving tomorrow?" She enquired.

"Yes"

"What have you thought? Do you want to take some time and then talk about it with your parents?"

"Nopes. I am pretty sure what I want. I am going to introduce her to my family today"

"But how? Don't you think you're running too fast?"

"Not at all. I think I am running with the wind. Wish me luck, buddy"

"You don't need to say this. My wishes are always with you, dear"

"Thanks, Shweta. I'll see you later"

"See you later. All the best, bye," and she hangs the call.

I immediately dialled the number of Sunaina.

"Hi, Sunaina; how are you?"

"Nothing. Just preparing my bags to return to Mumbai"

"I know you're angry with me, but I want to settle this on a pretty note tonight"

"First of all, who told you I am angry with you? I came so far to do my project, not to meet you" *It was a taunt. Beautiful girls are generally good at it.*

"Ok. Can we meet after an hour at your hotel?"

"For what?"

"To make this day memorable for you"

"I still remember that night, dude," she smiled softly. Thankfully, she was in a *good mood*.

"No, no, dear. I want to take you out shopping and a movie and dinner"

"Shall we meet at 12?"

"Done. I love you. Take care, bye"

"I love you too. See you at 12," *and she hangs the call.*

After that, I made some calls and made final arrangements. I prayed to God that things would go well.

Before I could put my feet down on the bed, I heard a knock on my door. It was Mom.

"Arjun, it's 9 in the morning. Do you need the whole day in your bed? Come down soon"

"I am coming in just 15 minutes." *I heard the footsteps sound heavy at first, but then slowly, the decibel level reduced. I knew Mom had left.*

I got ready in the next 20 minutes and came down for breakfast. My uncles were busy chatting about the financial market even on Sunday. I looked at my dad. His eyes were on me. We smiled, and I took my seat. Before anyone could say anything, I said with all my courage –

"I have something to say," *suddenly the financial market stopped. Ladies came out of the kitchen, looking at me. I guess my dad was aware of what I was about to say. His expression remained constant.*

"I want all of you to meet a girl tonight whom I have chosen as my life partner."

"We all know about it. We met her long ago," My aunt said.

*I was stunned but curious to know about it.*

"It's Shruti," My aunt says.

"Unfortunately, you're wrong. Her name is Sunaina. She is a Fashion Design student who lives in Mumbai."

"But how did you meet her, and why will we meet her tonight? Are we going to Mumbai, or is her family coming to Bangalore?" My uncle was more curious than my mom.

"No, uncle. She has been here in Bangalore for the past seven days. She had a project for which she chose Bangalore as a centre."

"Okay, so this story has been brewing for a long time," my aunt said, trying to pull my leg.

*I saw from the corner of my eye that my mom was standing near my dad's chair. She had not spoken a single word about it. She walked back to her room.*

"I'll be right back. But I want all of you to be ready. I will see you at 8:00 pm sharp at ITC Gardenia." Then I left to see Mom.

" May I come in, Mom?" I knocked on her door.

"You don't need to ask it" I came in and closed the door.

I went near her and sat on the ground

"Mom, I know you hate my choices, but believe me. This time I am not wrong. Sunaina is really a lovely girl. I am sure you would like her"

"What if I say No to your choice after I meet her?"

"First, I bet you won't say no to her. And if you did, I'll respect your words. I won't marry her, but I also promise I'll never marry any other girl too."

"So what's the point? Indirectly, you're asking me to take your side." *She was right. Only God knew how my dad handled her.*

"Mom, I really love her. I know you have the least faith in my choice, but please meet her once with an open heart. I am sure you would like her."

"I hope so."

"I'll see you in the evening," and left to meet Sunaina.

My heart was beating hard, and I was praying – Hopefully, Mom like Sunaina and accept her.

I was eagerly waiting for the evening. The whole day, I held Sunaina's hand. We went Shopping, had lunch, and then went to a movie. I dropped her off at the hotel and asked her to get ready for dinner.

After an hour, I came to receive her. She looked gorgeous in her fluorescent pink gown and knew how to carry herself. We left for ITC Gardenia.

As soon we reached the gates, the manager came down to receive us. He took us into a room which was nicely decorated with balloons. I was holding her hand, and we went inside the room. I looked at the manager, and he knew what he had to do next. He left the room and closed it slightly. I took Sunaina's hand in mine. I slowly whispered –

"I don't know how to thank you. In fact, the word 'thank you' is so inappropriate for what you did for me. From day 1, you made me smile. You showed me the way when I was heading towards the darkness. You brought a ray of hope in my dark life. I knew I was sounding too cheesy. But I really mean them from the bottom of my heart. Will you stay with me forever and take my surname as your last name?" I went on my knee with a Diamond ring.

"Yes, I would love to spend the rest of my life with you, Arjun," she said as she accepted the ring.

"Now, there is one more surprise for you." *Slowly, the gates opened after I made a clap. Our families came in together.*

"Mom, Dad, *Bhaiya,* how come you guys are here?" she was surprised.

"In the morning, Arjun gave us the call and said he wants us to be here tonight. He mailed us the tickets and made all the necessary arrangements so that we could reach here. He told us everything about you and himself. All the way, I thought about how this relationship would work in the future. But when I met his family, all my doubts vanished. I couldn't ask for more." Sunaina's dad came forward and hugged her. Her eyes went teary at that moment, but she was smiling all the time. I saw my mom and went near to her.

"I hope you like her."

"Don't worry this time. I met her parents. They were very simple and down-to-earth people. I think you made the right choice this time," I hugged my mom. It was a time for celebration. Our families accepted our relationship. It was a moment of joy. I knew she would be leaving the next day, but only to return to my life forever.

*After two years:*

We were married for almost one-and-half years. She opened up her boutique. I opened up my CA firm along with all my buddies – Ankit, Vikram, and Satyam. After all, they were also bored with slavery life.

Later, Ritz also joined us. Our team grew stronger. Shweta was well-settled in an MNC and worked as a senior manager in HR. Vicky and Shweta fixed their marriage dates after six months. Dad's business started running well. All his debts were paid off. Shruti met her perfect match and tied the knot within a year. I guess it was all that I wanted at the end – Happiness and prosperity all around.

www.ingramcontent.com/pod-product-compliance
Lightning Source LLC
LaVergne TN
LVHW041906070526
838199LV00051BA/2525